2/28

MW01154081

Anastasia's Diary
A Year in the Life of Anastasia Romanov
Duchess of Russia

Anastasia's Diary

Manufactured in the U.S.A
ISBN 978-1483989891
ISBN 1483989895

i

For Joy Sage
My little Princess

Anastasia's Diary

Other books by the author:

Nikola Tesla: A Spark of Genius
Agatha Christie: Writer of Mystery
Emily Dickinson: Singular Poet
Indira Gandhi: Daughter of India
Woodrow Wilson
William Shakespeare

Dear Reader:
Although the diary that you are about to read is a work of
fiction, the people and events described in its pages are real.

In the early 1900s, Russia was ruled by Tsar Nicholas
Romanov II and his wife, the Tsarina Alexandra. There were
also five children in the royal family: the Grand Duchesses
Olga, Tatiana, Marie, Anastasia and their younger brother, the
Tsarevitch Alexis.

The Romanov family was a close-knit group and the children
were doted on by their parents. The Grand Duchesses and
Alexis did not attend school but rather, tutors were engaged to
educate them. Their parents filled in the gaps with their own
life instruction.

At the time this diary begins, Russia is involved in a war with
Germany; the common people are becoming increasingly
unhappy about the way the country is being run; there are
signs of a revolution in the air; and the Royal family is being
blamed for the unrest in the country.

One of the disciplines that the Tsar and Tsarina passed on to
their daughters was the practice of keeping a diary. Both
monarchs wrote daily in their diaries and they encouraged
their daughters to do the same.

In 1917, just before the Revolutionaries moved the family to
their final destination, Ekaterinberg in Siberia, the Tsarina
gave her daughters an order; they were to burn all their diaries
for fear that the Revolutionaries find something written in the
journals that would jeopardize the future safety of the family.
This account is a fictionalized version of how fifteen-year-old

Anastasia's Diary

Anastasia's diary would have read if it had not been destroyed. It is my hope that after reading the following diary account, you will have a glimpse of what it was like to be the last Princess of Russia.

Anastasia's Immediate Family

Tsar (Czar) Nicholas II – father
Tsarina (Czarina) Alexandra – mother

Grand Duchesses Olga, Tatiana, Marie – older sisters
(*Duchess is the same as princess)
Tsarevitch (Csarevitch) Nikolay Alexandrovich (Alexis) –
younger brother and next in line to be Tsar. Alexis was a
hemophiliac, which means that he was prone to internal
bleeding whenever he injured himself. This situation was a
great worry to the family because Alexis came close to death
many times.

Other people mentioned in Anastasia's diary

Doctor Botkin – the family physician
Gleb and Tatiana Botkin – the doctor's children. They were
the only children, besides the Romanov cousins, who were
allowed to socialize with Anastasia and her sisters.

Captain Derevenko – the captain of the Standart, the Tsar's
yacht.

Pierre Gilliard – tutored Alexis in all subjects and tutored
Anastasia and her sisters in French. After the family was taken
prisoner in the palace, Gilliard took on the responsibility of
tutoring Anastasia and her sisters in all subjects.

Mademoiselle Tioutcheva – was governess to Anastasia and
her sisters.

Father Grigory Rasputin – a monk who exhibited
extraordinary healing powers. The Tsarina believed that Fr.
Grigory was sent by God in order to heal Alexis. The priest
was responsible for saving Alexis life many times. He
developed a bad reputation, however, and the Russian people
hated him. They believed that he was fooling the Tsarina into
believing that he was a holy man when in reality, he was evil.

Madame Schneider – tutored Anastasia and her sisters in
French.

Aunt Olga – the Tsar's younger sister.
Uncle Ernest – Frederick Ernst, Prince of Saxe-Altenburg
(Germany), the brother of the   Tsarina.
Uncle Felix – Prince Felix Felixsovich Youssoupov, from one
of the wealthiest families in Russia. He was married to the
Tsar's niece, Princess Irina. Anastasia and her sisters called
him "uncle", out of respect.
Aunt Elizabeth – Elizabeth Feodorovna, the Tsarina's sister
who was a nun.

Colonel Kerensky – one of the Revolutionaries in charge of
keeping the Royal family prisoners in the palace.
Colonel Kobylinsky – replaced Colonel Kerensky after a few
months.
Commissar Pankratoff – replaced Colonel Kobylinsky when
the family was moved to Siberia.

Places mentioned in the diary

Tsarkoe Selo (sometimes spelled Czsarkoe Selo and
pronounced "zaska sell o") – translates as "the Tsar's Village"
and it was where the Tsar's estate was located. It was about 15

miles south of St. Petersburg. In direct contrast to the surrounding monotonous, grey countryside, Tsarskoe Selo had parks, palaces, lakes and beautiful gardens. There were two palaces that the family frequented, the Catherine Palace and the Alexander's palace; the latter is the one in which the family lived most of the time.

The Tsar and Tsarina lived on the first floor and the children on the second floor with their nannies and tutors. The children had their own dining room, music room, classrooms and playrooms. There was also a movie theatre for Alexei. Although the Alexander Palace had about 200 rooms, it was not the largest palace on the estate.

Livadia – is located on the Black Sea in the Crimea. Tsar Nicolas built a luxurious palace there. It was Anastasia's favorite vacation spot.

Mohileff – a city in southern Russia. It served as the headquarters of the Russian army during the war and is referred to as "the Front".

[Author's note: the dates in the diary are written in the European style with the day first, then the month, and the year last (23 April 1917). I've kept to this style throughout the book as this is the way in which Anastasia would have written dates in her diary.]

1 October 1916

Dear Diary:

Last night, Mama handed me this beautiful daybook with a leather cover and my initials on the front. I just love it. The new pages crinkle deliciously when I fan them, and the soft leather feels like the skin on a short-haired cat. I decided to give you a name, Nina. You will be my best friend and my confidante. I will entrust all my secrets to you, and I know you will never tell anyone what I don't want them to know.

Things are so different now with Papa fighting in the war against Germany, and sometimes I don't feel like confiding my thoughts to Tatiana or Marie. Some of my feelings are a little embarrassing and I'm afraid that they will make fun of me, like the fact that I'm seriously in love with Gleb Botkin. If my sisters knew, they would tease me unmercifully and I couldn't stand to have my love for Gleb tainted by their jokes, Nina. I'll try to write to you every day.

Love, Anastasia

3 October 1916

Dear Nina,

Life just hasn't been the same since the war started. Papa is always leaving the palace to join his men at the Front, which is the worst part of this. Shivers of fear crawl up my skin when I think of how close he is to the fighting. But the second worse thing is that we will not be able to sail on Papa's yacht this summer. The Standart has been docked for many months, collecting barnacles on it hull, while its sailors fight in the war for Mother Russia. I know this is the selfish part of me coming out. I pray that it will soon be over.

5 October 1916

Sometimes I tire of the burden of being a duchess, Nina. It's all so formal. I must be on my best behavior in front of other people, even those in the palace. I may not have friends, except Gleb and Tatiana Botkin and my cousins who are terribly boring. Gleb and Tatiana need a formal invitation from Mama to visit the palace, which is rare. And my days are filled with tiresome lessons. But, I would especially like to be a commoner so that I could dream of marrying someone who I love rather than someone whom my parents think I should marry. All of our marriages will be arranged by Mama – we will have no choice in the matter of a husband.

I worry that Mama might choose some old duke for me to marry, with an ancient, wrinkled body and rheumy eyes. Ugh, how will I stand being with him? Or, if she chooses someone young, maybe he will be ugly and unkind, and I will not feel the spark of love that I see between Mama and Papa. How can I live with him and have his children??

This subject sometimes fills my mind and wakes me up at night, drenched in fear. It is a fact that my older sisters must be married first, so I don't have to worry for a few years yet. But, royal marriages are not like that of commoners. Royal alliances are usually made for political purposes, not for emotional ties. I just hope that when my time comes, Mama will be kind.

I told Gleb how I felt about my life when he and I were walking in the park today. As usual, we had to stop so he could draw a crow that was sitting on the branch of a tree.

He kept pushing a lock of his hair out of his eyes, so he could see clearly. I watched his hands while he sketched. He has the hands of a musician, not an artist, with long, thin fingers that could reach the lower notes on the piano quite easily.

"I've decided that I don't wish to be a princess anymore," I announced in my most matter-of-fact voice.

"Why, that's impossible, Your Highness. You are the daughter of the Tsar and Tsarina. You have no choice." He took up his pencil once again and resumed his drawing as if we had not spoken. "Besides," he said. "Lots of girls would be happy to trade places with you. I'm sure that you will change your mind when you grow up." Gleb is only two years older than I, but sometimes he speaks as if the difference in our ages is enormous.

"I'm sick of everyone telling me that I'll think differently when I'm grown. I really don't see why I should," I told him.

I angrily walked back to the palace with Tatiana and left him drawing his foolish crow.

Later: I see now that it was silly of me to lose my temper with Gleb. I enjoy his company so much and, except when we are traveling in the Crimea, we rarely get to be together and Gleb is such a wonderful friend. I shall send him a letter tomorrow. I will give it to Doctor Botkin and I will apologize for my immature behavior.

7 October 1916

Dear Nina,
I received a letter from Gleb today:

Your Highness,
Thank you for your letter of apology, however, it was
unnecessary. I am not angry with you. We are friends and
friends understand each other. I hope we will be able to walk
in the park again soon. I have enclosed the drawing of the
crow that we saw on our walk.
With deep respect,
Gleb Botkin

Needless to say, his lovely drawing is on the wall next to my bed, so it is the first thing I see in the morning and the last thing at night. He even wrote a note on it that says *"To her Highness Anastasia, from your friend, Gleb"*.

I am so glad to have you to share things with, Nina. I somehow feel that you really exist and it is only to you that I can open my heart and tell my most secret thoughts. Perhaps someday I will be able to have a husband with whom I can do the same. But I'll never let go of you, Nina. I'll just share with both of you.

8 October 1916

Dear Nina,

The weather is beautiful today with a fresh breeze blowing across the park and the remains of summer flowers displaying their final colors.

The war has changed many aspects of our life here at the palace, and one of the things that I miss the most is our pets who had to be sold in order to help with the costs of the war.

I brought my Kodak camera to the park today. I want pictures of everyone in the family. Mama is not a willing subject since I must pester and cajole her into posing for a photo, and she is usually not feeling well and spends a lot of time in her bedroom. Papa, on the other hand, will always sit for me when he is home, as will my sisters and Alexis although, Alexis doesn't really sit still for a pose. He has so much energy. So I have to catch him when he isn't looking and he stops to do something, like play with the toy soldiers on the table.

I asked Gleb to pose for a picture the other day and he became very embarrassed.

"Forgive me, Your Highness, but I do not like to have my photo taken. I feel uncomfortable in front of a camera."

I finally COMMANDED him to pose for me, so he couldn't refuse. Of course, my real reason for being so insistent was that I wished to have a photo of Gleb to keep under my pillow, to look at from time to time. He is quite handsome and I just know he would make a great husband. But, it's just not possible. Gleb and I would never be allowed to marry because of the difference in our status. Tatiana says that I must marry a grand duke or a prince in order to continue the royal line.

I don't understand why that is so important and neither do my sisters. They say that it 'just is'.

12 October 1916

Dear Nina,

The life of a princess can be a lonely one at times, so I'm very happy to have you to share things with. As Grand Duchesses, we are not allowed close friends, for there is no one who is worthy to be our companions. Only when we visit Livadia in the Crimea, are restrictions lifted somewhat and Gleb and Tatiana can join us in games. However, we haven't taken a trip on the Standart in some time, and I miss all the fun we used to have.

I do have my cousins, of course. Most of them are so boorish that I can't tolerate being with them for more than a few hours.

My sisters and I must always be chaperoned wherever we go, even to the park on the palace grounds. Either Mme. Schneider or Mama's lady-in-waiting is constantly with us in the park and their voices drone on with the dangers of doing "this" and the chances that we will be hurt doing "that". If we injure ourselves, even to the slightest scratch on our finger, they must answer to Mama.

Captain Derevenko has charge of chaperoning Alexis. Since Alexis is so delicate and even the most minor injury can threaten his life, Captain Derevenko must be by his side constantly, in case Alexis should trip or fall and his bleeding begin again.

I'd give anything to have a REAL friend!

15 October 1916

Dear Nina,

We are traveling on Papa's train to Mohileff [in Russia] where Papa is stationed at the Front. This is very exciting for all of us, not only because we will see Papa again, but because we are actually taking a vacation away from the palace, which we have not done in a long time.

I remember in years past, before the war, when the summer months were spent in Livadia, near Finland. We would sail on Papa's yacht and spend our days lying on the deck feeling the warm sun on our faces. Papa and Mama would relax in their deckchairs while Captain Derevenko and Admiral Papa-Federov would take charge of the boat. Sometimes we would stop at one of the islands to hike over the rocky terrain. Other times the Standart would anchor a mile or so from shore. Papa, in a short-sleeved top which displayed his tan arms, would row us to one of the islands where we could swim and play in the water until our skin started to wrinkle. Oh, how I miss those times. Olga told me that Mama said, "Next year, when the war is over, we can spend part of the year in Livadia." I CAN'T WAIT!!

16 October 1916

Dearest Nina,

We finally reached Mohileff today. Oh, what a joyous reunion it was! Papa looks tired but his face lit up when he saw us.

It was raining today so we remained on the train. Papa's train, with its twelve cars, is so large, that we don't feel confined in the least. Our daily routine goes on as usual, including our lessons! Some vacation, Nina, when we must take our studies with us! And Mama made sure that we all brought our needlework with us. How I HATE to do cross-stitch! I keep pricking my fingers with the needle and I'm so bored the entire time.

Nina, Papa hasn't been able to spend much time with us, except at dinner. He says that he has a "mountain of duties" that he must attend to.

I know that he expects that we will forgive him for not spending more time with us, but I don't understand. Our whole lives are centered on this stupid war and I'm sick of it, Nina. I just want it to be over NOW!

18 October 1916

Nina,

I am so sad to be on our way back home to Tsarkoe Selo. Mama was crying when she kissed Papa good-bye and he gave us all a great hug and promised that he will come home to us just as soon as it is possible.

Monsieur Gilliard went on holiday for a couple of weeks so we will be without a French tutor after we arrive home. This is quite to my liking. However, Mama insists that we spend at least one hour each day with our French reader in addition to the assignments that Monsieur Gilliard left for us.

It is difficult to read even for an hour. My mind quickly goes back to the countryside; there is so much to see while traveling. Miles and miles of green fields, some of them plowed under after the summer harvest, many of them not used at all. I saw the tiny houses of the peasants, many of them with children playing outside. As we passed a small river, I noted some women washing their clothes in the icy cold water. I imagine their hands red and blistered with cold after their chores are done.

19 October 1916

Dear Nina,

Today we stopped and visited with some of the people in the neighboring villages near Mohileff. Everyone was so happy to meet us. They bowed and scraped to Mama and my hand was kissed so much that I thought the skin would rub off. We brought sweets for the children while the people gave us gifts of food and wine.

In one village, I met a young girl who was my age. Her name was Babka. She and I became friends and when Mama was distracted I thought that I'd show her around the train.

I felt so special because she was so impressed with Papa's train. She confided in me that she always wanted to be a princess. It was then that I told her that I always wanted to be a peasant girl. Well, not always. But I didn't tell her that. Then I showed her how my sisters and I sometimes sunbathed on the floor of Papa's study.

We were lying there, sharing secrets, when Mama came in. She was as surprised by us as we were by her. Poor Babka. She jumped up from the floor and bowed so low to Mama that she nearly fell on her face. I had to stifle a giggle even though I could see the anger in Mama's eyes.

She was not happy about finding us there, but as the Empress of Russia, she must maintain her dignity at all times.

"Ana, I'm sure this young lady is being sought by her parents. Please do not detain her any longer."

Babka nearly flew out the door of the car before I could even say good-bye. I braced myself for a lecture from Mama. I know that I will be punished for my insensitivity.

Nina, I see nothing wrong in wanting to talk to someone other than my sisters. How I wish I could change places with Babka, if only for a day.

25 October 1916

Life at the palace has returned to normal, Nina. Mama, Olga and Tatiana spend most of their day at the Catherine Palace hospital tending to the wounded soldiers. Since they all have their certificate in nursing, they are able to do a great deal of good there. Marie and I, although too young to do any serious nursing, try to visit the hospital whenever possible. The men cheer up when we arrive. They have even renamed the hospital, the Anastasia Marie Hospital!

Sometimes, I sing and dance, if they ask me. Other times we just talk. They always have so many questions about my life in the palace, Nina. They make my life seem so special, when really, it's not. I'd much rather experience the freedom and adventure of a soldier's life, than be confined to a boring lifetime of lessons and manners.

Oh, by the way, Mama decided not to punish me for asking Babka into Father's study. But I did get a long lecture...ugh!

27 October 1916

Dear Nina,

Papa has returned home again safely. He has brought one of the wounded men with him on his private train. Captain Felix Dassel of the 9th Kagar Dragoons of the Grand Duchess Olga was hit in the leg by schrapnel. Papa suggested that Marie and I meet Captain Dassel on our visit to the hospital today.

We arrived to find that an army cot had been placed in one of the rooms due to the shortage of a bed. Mama had made sure that Captain Dassel was comfortable. He seemed to be quite pale and weak but he made an effort to raise himself up on his elbow to kiss our hands.

He is an exceedingly handsome man with dusty brown hair and light blue eyes, like mine. Marie and I tried to distract Captain Dassel until Doctor Volkov could arrive to remove the metal from his leg, so I asked him questions about his family.

Captain Dassel lives in a small village in the South of Russia called Mitzkov. There, his mother, wife and three small children await his return from the war. He told us that he worries about them all the time because there is no male in the family to care for the women except an old and feeble uncle who lives nearby.

I told Captain Dassel that I would ask Mama for her help in getting a letter to his family so they would know that he was in the best of care in the palace hospital.

29 October 1916

Dear Nina,

Papa is leaving for the Front again, after spending only two days at home. We are all so sad, but Mama, most of all. She was hardly able to control her tears when Papa told her that he was to leave again. He is Commander-in-Chief and feels an immense responsibility to be with his soldiers while they are fighting for his beloved Russia.

Mama and Papa are so much in love. They write to each other every day when Papa is away. Long letters which I can only guess the contents of. I hope that when I marry, I will love my husband as deeply as Mama loves Papa.

I have read that not all unions are as true. Lots of people, especially those of royal blood, marry for reasons other than love. I don't think these unions can be very happy, as the couple will soon tire of each other and then living together will be dreadfully boring.

I hope this is not the situation that I will find myself in when I marry since Mama must choose my husband. How am I to love him when I don't even know him?

I've also read that a husband can be very demanding and that the wife must do as he commands. I don't think this is a fair arrangement, nor do I think that I would be able to be at another's command.

4 November 1916

Dear Nina,

Listen to this! "I think Gleb loves you, Ana." That's what Tatiana said to me this morning while we were sitting on our beds preparing to dress. I felt as if an electric shock touched my heart.

"He kissed your hand, yesterday," said Olga. "and everyone knows that he hates to kiss ladies' hands."

"And he draws pictures just for you," said Marie.

Is it possible that Gleb does love me? I would just die if he really did. But how could he? I'm not pretty like Marie and Tatiana, or as smart as Olga. But I don't think I'm ugly.

Later: I sneaked into Mama's dressing room today to see myself in her looking glass.

I saw a fifteen-year-old girl who was not very tall, but who probably has a couple of years left to grow. She has a few more pounds than she needs, but that's probably due to her passion for chocolates. This Grand Duchess has light brown hair which is fine and very soft. Her eyes are quite blue and everyone says that they are just like Papa's eyes.

So, perhaps I am not quite as comely as Tatiana, but Gleb thinks I'm pretty and that's all that matters.

6 November 1916

Dearest Nina,

I must grow taller so that Gleb will like me more. Yesterday, during our walk in the park, he called me "little Duchess" and I realized for the first time that he almost always refers to me with the word "little" in front of my title.

It makes me very angry because he is not much older than I am, yet what makes the difference is his height. Gleb is tall, almost as tall as Papa; therefore, everyone thinks that he is older than his years. If I were taller, Gleb would think of me as being older than my fifteen years and he would begin to think of me as a woman instead of as a little girl.

When Doctor Botkin, Gleb's father, came to minister to Mama this morning (she is suffering with terrible headaches), I asked him how many years I had left in which to grow taller. He said that I would probably stop growing when I was sixteen years old. How frightening!

That means that I am left with little less than a year during which I must add considerable inches to my height. I think that it would be foolish of me to trust nature to this task, so I've decided to do something about it myself. With this resolve in mind I thought of Captain Derevenko. His is one of Papa's sailors and is well over six feet tall. Tomorrow when his son arrives to play with Alexis, I will ask him how he managed to grow so tall.

7 November 1916

I've got the secret! Captain Derevenko shared it with me today but he made me promise that I wouldn't tell anyone else, so I'm writing it to you, Nina, because I know my secret will be safe. This is what he told me:

"When I was a young man, there lived in my town of Golnik, an old gypsy woman. Each week, people came from neighboring towns to have their fortunes told or to get herbal remedies for their ailments because good doctors like Doctor Botkin were almost never to be seen.

One day, when I was about thirteen years old, my mother visited this esteemed gypsy woman to ask her for an herbal remedy which would make me grow tall. Since everyone in my family was less than five feet and nine inches, my mother wanted to break the tradition and have a tall son. The gypsy woman did not provide my mother with herbs, however. Instead, she told her of a method which she swore was proven time and again for stimulating the growth glands in young people.

She told my mother that I was to hop around the dining room table on one foot for as long as I could keep it up. Then, I was to change feet and continue hopping around the table until exhaustion set in. The old woman instructed my mother to encourage me to do this daily until I reached the height of my desire."

Captain Derevenko is now more than six feet and two inches tall, a height which I have no desire to reach. It simply means that I won't have to hop for as long as time as he did.

I am so excited to learn of this secret method, and can't wait to begin practicing tomorrow.

8 November 1916

I began to practice today, Nina. After lunch, when everyone was about their own business and just before I began my lessons, I went into the dining room with the intention of following Captain Derevenko's instructions.

When all the servants had left and the room was empty, I began to hop on one leg around the table. When my right leg got too tired, I changed to my left leg. I promised myself that I will do this everyday for one month. Surely after this time I will have grown at least one or two inches taller.

9 November 1916

Nina,

My legs hurt terribly today. I first felt the pain when I arose from bed this morning.

Marie noticed that I winced when I tried to walk and she was about to call Mama, but I stopped her just in time. I laughed and told her that I was just fooling and that everything was alright and she believed me. By the afternoon walk in the park, my legs felt better and I was even able to do my hopping exercise, but only for a few minutes.

I think I would die of shame if anyone were to discover what I am doing.

12 November 1916

Oh, Nina,

I feel like a real ninny. I was hoping around the dining room table today, when I looked up to see Doctor Botkin watching me.

I stopped immediately. I could feel my face get hot with embarrassment.

"What in the world are you doing, your Highness?"

"I can't tell you," I answered.

"Why not? Is it a secret?" Doctor Botkin asked.

"Yes, a secret between Captain Derevenko and myself," I told him.

"Captain Derevenko? Ah, yes. Now I understand," Doctor Botkin chuckled. "He didn't happen to tell you the story about the gypsy woman and her technique for growing taller?"

I didn't have to respond because Doctor Botkin saw the answer in my face and he started to laugh.

"You must be wary of Captain Derevenko's stories. He is a grand storyteller and can make almost anyone believe his tales. But don't feel so embarrassed, your Highness, you are not the first person to be fooled by Captain Derevenko's advice."

"But I was afraid that I wouldn't grow as tall as Olga and Tatiana," I told him.

"Your Highness, with all due respect, your height and the build of your body is determined at birth and there is nothing that one can do to change that. You will grow as you are destined to grow and you must accept that as God's will. There have been many great women in history who have not been much taller than five feet, but that did not stop them from ruling countries and wielding tremendous power. A person's power comes from their inner growth, not from their outer growth."

I asked Doctor Botkin to keep my secret and he promised that he would. But I am angry at Captain Derevenko.

14 November 1916

Dear Nina,

Alexis is quite ill again. He fell today while playing with Captain Derevenko's son and Mama says that he is bleeding inside his body. This happens whenever he hurts himself.

Papa has been notified and so has Father Grigory Rasputin. In the past, he is the only one who has been able to make Alexis better. I pray that he will be able to perform a miracle on him again.

I can usually make Alexei feel better with my jokes and dances, but right now he is too ill to even recognize me. Oh, I don't know what I will do if he dies!

16 November 1916

Father Grigory arrived this morning and spent several hours with Mama and Alexis; he stopped Alexis's bleeding! He is truly a godly man because he can work miracles.

When he left, Mama had a wonderful smile on her face and hurried to send Papa a telegram telling him the good news.

17 November 1916

Dear Nina,

Mama hasn't left Alexis' side for days although he is feeling better. I never forget to thank God for sending Father Grigory to us. He has not only healed Alexis on several occasions, but Mama has gone to him many times for solace and comfort during this very difficult time that the country has been going through. He has given her a great deal of advice which she interprets as coming from God himself through Father Grigory's mouth and Mama always follows his guidelines.

However, there are many people in the palace and in Russia who do not think well of our Good Friend and think that he is a charlatan. At least, that is what Olga whispered to us the other night, when we all gathered in my and Marie's bedroom. She said that a charlatan is someone who pretends to be something he is not. She said that many people say that Father Grigory is very evil and unchristian, and some even say that he is the devil himself.

Then, Olga told us that some people believe that we are his love mistresses. We got a good laugh over that one!! We were laughing so hard, our eyes were tearing up and we were rolling on the beds holding our stomachs. Olga kept reminding us to be quiet, but it was almost impossible for us to stop laughing.

When I asked Olga how she knew all of this, she said that one of the soldiers in the hospital who had grown fond of her told her everything. He felt that Olga should know what people were saying about Father Grigory so that she would not be fooled into believing that he is a holy man when he is really a sinner.

We all decided that this soldier must have been taken in by the terrible rumors the jealous people started because they did not like the fact that our Good Friend is a favorite at the palace. People can be very vicious in their lies and accusations and I'm sure that this is what has happened.

19 November 1916

Dear Nina,

I miss Gleb terribly. Now that the weather is so cold, we no longer take walks in the park and I have no chance of seeing him. I do have his photo and I've taken to sleeping with his picture under my pillow at night. This makes me feel closer to him. DOES HE STILL LOVE ME?

20 November 1916

What fun, Nina! We have decided to write and perform our own play! Marie and I will write it and Tatiana and Olga will perform it with us. They spend long hours at the hospital, so they don't have the time to write it.

Marie reminded me that, before the war, we used to perform plays all the time for Mama and Papa. We often invited Aunt Olga and Doctor Botkin to watch and everyone had a wonderful time. Since the war began, almost two years ago, Papa has been away a good deal of the time and we don't feel like performing when he is not here to see it. But now we have decided to write a play and perform it for the soldiers at the Catherine Palace Hospital. Then, when Papa returns home, we will perform it for him.

We will begin writing tonight and not let anyone see the play until after it is written!

21 November 1916

Nina,

Alexis is healing and Mama sent a note of thanks to Father Grigory for his help. Doctor Botkin allowed us to visit with our little brother today, but only for a few minutes. He tires quite easily now.

22 November 1916

Nina,

It's a grand day for Captain Dassel. He is finally well enough to leave the hospital, although he will walk with a slight limp for awhile. He is planning to go home for a week before returning to the Front.

Last week, Captain Dassel asked if we would agree to take a photo of him sitting next to Marie and myself because "my Sasha will never believe that I was tended to by the Grand Duchesses themselves." We thought that was great fun and asked one of the other patients to take the photo. I had the roll of film developed immediately so that the Captain could have his photo when he left.

So he was surprised and delighted when Marie and I presented him with a gift: a gold medallion which we give to all of the men on the day they leave the hospital, and the photo which we had taken last week. Captain Dassel was very touched by all of this and he held our hands an extraordinarily long time after kissing them.

Marie and I will miss Captain Dassel as we miss most of the patients who we tend to in the hospital. We grow very fond of them and they of us, and it is always a small ache in my heart when one of the soldiers leaves. Especially because I know that most of them are going back to fight in the war and many may never return to their loved ones.

War is a horrible thing and history has been filled with wars, at least that is what Mademoiselle Tioutcheva tells us. I care very little for history; she is constantly calling my attention back to the lesson.

Sometimes, I wonder what it would be like if women were the rulers of the world instead of men. Men have ruled the world for so long and have made such a mess of things with

25

wars and fighting all the time. I think it's because men long for such aggressive occupations that they do not try hard enough to avoid conflicts. For what else would armies and military men do if there were no wars to fight?

Women, on the other hand, do not like wars, nor do they like bloodshed and fighting. I think that women rulers would try to avoid war at all costs and perhaps they would be more amenable to sitting down and trying to work things out. Perhaps when I grow up there will be more women rulers and we will cease to send our men off to war to be killed.

24 November 1916

Our play is going well and it is ever so much fun to write. It is difficult to have time to write it though, because we want to keep it a surprise, so we must write after Mama thinks we are asleep.

I stole a candle from the sideboard in the dining room the other day. Now, after Mama says goodnight to us, Tatiana and Olga sneak into our room and we discuss the play. Marie writes everything down as we go along, since she has the finest handwriting of all of us.

We haven't yet thought about a title for our play but we do have a story. It is about three sisters who are orphans and get taken in by a countess. They think that they have happened upon good fortune but they don't know that the countess is very evil and she wants to make the girls her slaves. When the sisters discover the countess' intentions, they plan a method of escape.

That is about as far as we've gotten with the story, Nina, but we are having a conflict with the parts. Everyone wants to play the evil countess and we started to argue over who would get the choice part. My sisters think that I'm too young to make a convincing countess. The part will probably go to Olga, since she is the oldest.

I'm sure this will be one of the finest plays we have ever performed.

28 November 1916

Madame Schneider is a stuffy old biddy!

Olga showed our play to her and she has gone to Mama to beg her not to allow us to perform it. Olga said that Madame Schneider was very upset after reading the play. She objects to the fact that we have an evil countess in the play and she thinks this is quite improper.

We are all angry with Olga for showing our play to Madame Schneider. It was supposed to be kept a secret until the night of our performance and now she has ruined it all.

"But I thought Madame Schneider could help us with the play," Olga told us when we accused her of breaking our bond of secrecy. We are all so ANGRY with her.

Of course, Mama must abide by the wishes of Madame Schneider because, as she told us: "I have given her the authority to teach you what is proper, since she, herself, is a lady of delicate manners and great sensitivity. I must, therefore, honor her advice on what is appropriate behavior for my daughters. So, I must ask you to write a more suitable play."

Later: Olga is very contrite about what she did and we have all forgiven her, but we decided to wait awhile before writing another play. Perhaps by then, Madame Schneider will be replaced by a tutor who is not quite so boorish and we will be able to write the sort of play that we want to.

29 November 1916

Dear Nina,

I'm so excited! I finally know what to do with my life when I get older. I want to be an actress!

I had a dream last night in which I was performing on the stage and everyone was applauding me. I felt so, so special.

I must tell Mama what I intend to do. Perhaps she will arrange for a drama tutor to teach me, so when I'm older, I will be ready to perform on a real stage.

1 December 1916

Nina, I feel as if a sword has pierced my heart and it is shattering even as I write. After two days of walking around in a daze of future dreams about being on the stage, Mama has crushed my dream in an instant.

I had been anxious to speak with Mama and it was difficult to find her alone. Thus, when I knocked on the door of her sitting room today and found her alone, my excitement mounted and I couldn't wait to speak.

The words tumbled out of my mouth as I told her about my dream the other night and my wish to be an actress. As I finished sharing my news, I noticed that Mama's face had turned quite pale. She pulled me down beside her on the settee and took my hand.

"Ana, you must give up this silly notion of yours immediately," she said. "You are a Grand Duchess, a member of the Russian nobility. You could never become an actress. It is one of the lowliest of professions and hardly befitting a young woman of your background."

I could feel my hot tears welling up into my eyes and I was afraid that they would spill over at any moment. I didn't wish Mama to see me crying like a baby.

"But Mama, before the war, you and Papa used to go to the Minsky Theatre to see Madame Trotsky perform and you all applauded her. You even invited her to a dinner here at the palace in her honor."

"Ana, that is a very different situation. We might admire Madame Trotsky for her acting ability, but she is not of royal blood. If she were, I can assure you that she would not have become an actress."

"What am I to do when I am grown?" I asked Mama.

"Your role in life, Ana, is to be the wife of a very special man, chosen by Papa and myself when the time is ready. Perhaps you will be betrothed to a count or to a prince. Being a wife and mother is the most elevated occupation for a young woman to aspire to."

I could say nothing more than, "Yes, Mama."

As I was about to take my leave, Mama stopped me.

"Ana, please don't tell your sisters about this silly idea. I don't want their heads filled with such notions."

2 December 1916

Dear Nina,

There is an empty feeling in the bottom of my stomach and in my heart. It is as if one spent days awaiting a heart's desire and in a minute, one finds that it will never come to pass. NEVER! NEVER!

I try to play the piano but I have no heart for it. Tatiana and Marie tried to engage me in a game of tennis, but I don't want to do that either. I have no tolerance for my lessons either. I want to burn my books because I absolutely HATE learning.

I wonder if Mama knows how sad she has made me with her decision. I wonder now what the purpose of my life is. Why should God give me talents if I'm never to use them? Why did I have the misfortune to be born a princess instead of a person of common station, free to do whatever I choose with my life?

5 December 1916

Dearest Nina,

I am sorry that you have been neglected these few days. I haven't felt like doing much of anything, not even writing. However, I felt better when I awoke this morning. It seems the heavy sorrow that I felt last week is finally lifting.

I realize that it doesn't do any good to moan and cry over something that I have no control over. I have no control over my future life, and I must just accept that as God's will – and Mama's.

I must confess that I did not come to this understanding on my own but rather with the help of Marie in whom I confided my secret desire. She told me that as Grand Duchess and daughter of the Tsar, there are very few choices that I can make for my future. She said that there are two: to be a wife and mother or to enter the convent, like Aunt Elizabeth. I didn't have to think too long upon which choice I would make.

6 December 1916

Dear Nina,

I have a secret to share with you! Uncle Ernest arrived from Germany this morning to visit Papa. He was closeted with Papa in his study for a very long time. Before he left, Uncle Ernest visited with us, also. He is Mama's brother and was especially happy to see Mama since they hadn't seen each other since the war with Germany began.

Uncle Ernest brought presents for all of us. I received a scarf with the initial "A" embroidered on it and when I put it around my neck, it felt soft as cotton. Mama said that it is made of cashmere, one of the finest wools.

Mama told us to be mum about seeing Uncle Ernest, so I am telling you, dear Nina. I suppose the reason is that we are at war with Germany and if anyone in Germany found out that Uncle Ernest was here, he would be in a great deal of trouble. Also, if others found out that we were meeting with a high-ranking German, the Russian people would be very upset; they would think we were giving secrets to the German army. Mama says that there could be spies here in the palace, so we must not talk of the visit, even among ourselves.

Later:

Olga discovered the reason for Uncle Ernest's visit. He came to ask Papa to consider making peace with Germany, thereby ending the war. Papa refused!

7 December 1916

Dearest Nina,
Papa left for the Front again. I HATE THIS WAR!!

9 December 1916
Mama invited Monsieur Gilliard to dine with us. After we had
finished dinner, we all joined Mama in her sitting room for
tea. There was a sense of tranquility that was felt by everyone.
Olga and Tatiana were busy knitting woolen socks for the
soldiers, while Marie and I practiced our needlepoint.

Mama queried Monsieur Gilliard for what seemed forever,
about Alexis' lessons and the progress he is making.
Monsieur exhibited a great deal of patience when answering
Mama's questions and Alexis was the subject of their
discussion for well over an hour. Only one thing made me sad
– the absence of Papa. I pray that this war might be over soon
so that we can be a family again.

10 December 1916

Dear Nina,

I am trying to finish making my Christmas gifts. I am tatting a pillow cover for Mama and for Papa I have a picture frame with a photo of all of us that he can take to the Front with him. I had Captain Derevenko take the photo for me. I have embroidered handkerchiefs for each of my sisters, and for Alexis, I knitted a wool scarf.

I love Christmas! The anticipation of that wondrous day with all the preparations and love that goes into each gift, makes it the most special day of the year (besides my birthday, of course). And I am not the only one who is busy making presents. It is the one time of the year when we allow each other alone-time in which to work on our gifts. We all want to be surprised, so not one of us tries to intrude on the other.

Only fifteen more days! I CAN'T WAIT!!

11 December 1916

Dearest Nina,

Mama thinks that we are very sheltered, but we are actually privy to many things that go on, both in and outside of the palace. It is Olga who is our primary informant. She makes it a point to walk by the kitchen as often as possible. Here, Cook and the other servants chatter and gossip about all they see and hear during the day.

It was in this way that we learned today that our governess, Mademoiselle Tioutcheva was let go. She said something terrible to Mama about Father Grigory. She asked Mama to arrange that our Good Friend not be allowed to come near our rooms to speak to us. Mama became enraged at this suggestion, and told Mademoiselle to leave the palace immediately.

A short while after Olga gave us this news, Mama came to our rooms.

"I have decided that you girls no longer have need of a governess," she told us. "Therefore, I have dismissed Mademoiselle. She was anxious to return to her family so she was unable to see you before she left. She has asked me to bid you all a fond good-bye in her place." At that, Mama turned and left the room.

It was hard not to let on to Mama that we knew the real truth of this matter. It is true that we will all miss her; however, I applaud Mama's action in letting go of Mademoiselle. Father Grigory is a holy man of God and it was not proper that our governess should speak ill of him.

Later: Oh, Nina, I kiss Gleb's photo every morning. Yesterday, I tried to talk to Doctor Botkin about him, but the doctor was in a hurry and all he could tell me was that Gleb was studying for his final examinations. Oh, how I wish we could all go to Livadia again – we had the best time of our lives there!

13 December 1916

Our Good Friend, Father Grigory is dead, Nina!

I can hardly believe that I am actually telling you this. It seems as if I will awake at any moment from a terrible dream and find out that none of this is true.

A messenger came to the palace early this morning to give Mama the news. She is overcome with grief and has taken to her rooms. Doctor Botkin is with Mama now, helping her to steady her nerves.

We are all shaken by this tragedy. We all held each other and cried our eyes out when Doctor Botkin told us. It seems that all we hear lately is unhappy news and I don't quite know what to make of it all.

Later: Tatiana told me that she overheard Cook talking with one of the servants and they were discussing Father Grigory's death. Tatiana learned that he had been poisoned while dining with Uncle Felix. He was then shot several times when he tried to escape the house. The police found his body floating in the St. Petersburg Canal this morning. HOW HORRIBLE!

I wish I hadn't been privy to all the details of Father Grigory's death. We have seen much death while working in the hospital and attended many funerals, but the death of our Good Friend has affected us all deeply.

I am convinced that Father Grigory was a good man, contrary to all the villainous things that have been said about him. He was Mama's strength and support, and Alexis, poor dear Alexis. What will we do now if he begins to bleed? Father Grigory will not be here to heal his wounds and make the bleeding stop. I must have a serious talk with Alexis. He must realize that he cannot do everything that others do. His life is in mortal danger!

14 December 1916

Dear Nina,

Mama finally came out of her room today. Her face was still red from weeping and she walked with a great effort, even with the aid of her cane. The shock of our Good Friend's death must have made her arthritis worse.

She called all of us together to tell us that she wrote to Papa telling him to come home immediately. Mama also told us that she has asked Papa to arrest Uncle Felix for Father Grigory's murder. She said that Uncle Felix had been seen last month marching with the Bolshevik workers, and everyone knows that they hated Father Grigory as they hate our whole family.

We were silent as we listened to Mama tell us these things and none of us said a word that we already knew the details of Father Grigory's death. Tatiana had sworn us to secrecy, for Mama would be horrified to learn that her daughters were privy to such shocking details. She would be sure that it would disturb us terribly, which it has.

The only good thing that has come of all this is that Papa will be coming home. I miss him with all my heart and I get lonely sometimes when he is not here.

15 December 1916

Last night I had a frightening dream, Nina. A true nightmare!

I dreamed that I was swimming in the St. Petersburg Canal when I saw Father Grigory swimming toward me. I was shocked, because even in my dream I knew that he was dead. As he approached, I could see him more clearly and I screamed out in terror at the ghastly features of his face. There was a huge hole in his forehead! I immediately realized that he was not the kindly friend that I knew, but an evil creature who meant to kill me.

I turned and swam as fast as I could, but found that I was rooted to the same spot in the water, no matter how I exerted my arms. Suddenly, I felt a hand on my dress collar and felt myself being pulled under the water, as I kicked and struggled to get free. I awoke to find Marie pulling on my nightdress in an attempt to awaken me.

After sharing the dream with her, I felt a little better. In telling Marie about it, it seemed more a dream and less a reality. However, I was afraid that I would resume the dream again as soon as I fell back to sleep.

Oh, Nina, I was so afraid. I made Marie promise me that she would wake me again if she heard me cry out. But I lay there for the longest time snuggling against the warmth of Marie's back until I finally fell asleep.

16 December 1916

Dearest Nina,

Today we said good-bye to our Good Friend for the last time. Mama arranged to have Father Grigory's body buried in a corner of the park here at Tsarkoe Selo. It is such a bleak day, well suited for a funeral, I suppose, with an occasional misty rain settling upon our hair and mourning black clothing. Even Alexis was in his formal clothes. At 10 o'clock this morning, we joined Mama at the gravesite where we said prayers along with Father Nickolai. Mama made sure that we all wore our lockets with Father Grigory's picture inside.

Before we left the grave, I overheard Mama say something strange, almost as if to herself. She said that she always knew that the end would be near when Father Grigory went to heaven. I asked Mama what she meant by that, but she said, "Nothing, my dear Ana. Nothing."

Mama looked frightened and pale and her words have left a feeling of foreboding in my mind. We all believe that Mama has the gift of sight sometimes and it is this that frightens me. Will it be the end of the world? The end of the Russian empire? Or the end of the Romanov family?

18 December 1916

Dear Nina,

Papa came home last night and we are a family again. This is what makes us all very happy.

I went to the hospital again today after lessons. Mama missed several days after the death of Father Grigory, but Olga and Tatiana went to do Mama's work along with their own. Marie and I sometimes play chess or checkers with the soldiers. I'm not very good at chess but I can beat most of the soldiers at checkers, except the "Man with the Pockets".

I call him that because whenever he greets me, he always has his hands in his pockets. He must know that it is disrespectful to address me in this fashion, yet he continues anyway. I have been hesitant to tell anyone for fear that he will be reprimanded for it.

20 December 1916

Nina,

I am feeling so miserable today, even though the sun is shining bright and Papa is home with us. I just want to cry over everything. I'm sure it has to do with my monthlies which are coming on. Mama says that God gave women this monthly curse as punishment for the sins of Eve.

I HATE this war, Nina. I HATE not having any friends, except you, to talk with. I HATE that Papa is away all the time and that our lives are so different. And I'm scared! Olga told us today that there is talk of an overthrow of Papa as ruler! Monsieur Gilliard, however, said that it was probably not possible.

21 December 1916

Dear Nina,

We are finishing our last minute preparations for Christmas. The New Year's tree is decorated and stands at least eight feet tall in the hallway and those who have finished their presents have placed them under the tree already.

The only sadness this Christmas is the death of our Good Friend, which is still in our minds and hearts. Mama, especially, has not been herself since the tragedy happened.

23 December 1916

Mama and Papa had an argument. I was about to enter Mama's drawing room when I heard Papa's voice talking very loud. I know it was dreadful of me to listen, Nina, but I couldn't help it. Mama and Papa never argue, so I felt that this must be terribly important.

Mama said that she was still in mourning for Father Grigory and she didn't feel that it was right that she should be present for holiday celebrations. Papa, who didn't feel as close to our Good Friend, told Mama that, as Empress, it was her duty to greet our guests and be a joyful hostess to all who will arrive at the court. He said that her feelings for Father Grigory must not interfere with our Christmas celebration. In the end, Mama will have no choice but to do as Papa wishes.

Later: Although Mama is German and English, our Christmas celebrations have always been conducted according to the Russian tradition. Cook and the servants have been busy for weeks baking pastries, cookies, and sweets to serve to the court guests who will arrive tomorrow on Holy Night and on Christmas day.

The baker also makes wheat cakes for St. Nicholas. Tomorrow, Nina, we will put them on the windowsills. When St. Nicholas or Kolya was alive, he used to leave money on the windowsills of the homes of poor people while they were sleeping at night, but we leave wheat cakes instead.

Marie and I ran around the palace tonight, singing our favorite Christmas song:

Kolya, Kolya,
On Christmas Eve, when all is still,
He puts his cakes on the windowsill.
Kolya, Kolya,
Come this Holy Night, we pray,
Come and bring us Christmas day!

24 December 1916

Dear Nina,

Every year, when we were young, we would join Mama in her sitting rooms and while we were served tea and pastries, she would tell us the story of Babushka. We had to beg Mama to continue this tradition that we all love so much, and she finally agreed.

There is a legend that Babushka, which means grandmother in Russian, was very unkind and she refused shelter to the Holy Family on its way to Egypt. However, before she died she repented and ever since, she has tried to make up for her unkindness to the Holy Child by giving presents to children on Christmas Eve. When we were little, we believed that Babushka brought us the presents that we found under the New Year's tree.

We will go to midnight Mass in a couple of hours. Anyone who is at the court will be invited to go with us. Then, when we return, Papa will give a traditional blessing. But the best part is the pastries and cakes that follow. Last year, I got sick from eating too many of them.

25 December 1916

'S Rozhdestvom Khristovym, Nina! What a wonderful Christmas Day! Everyone was in such a joyful mood that it had its effect on Mama. Her spell of sadness was broken with all the happiness that everyone felt today.

I received many gifts from guests who came to the palace these two days, but those from my family were the best. From Papa and Mama, I received a pair of earrings. A knitted shawl from Tatiana. An embroidered diary cover from Olga, a scarf from Marie and a bookmark from Alexis.

Gleb sent me a box of Swiss chocolates. He knows how much I love them. I think that I'm going to be selfish and hide them under my bed so that they will last a long time.

I was enjoying this day so much that I even forgot there was a war going on until we went to the hospital to give our Christmas tidings to the soldiers there. Many of them were very glum and not at all into the Christmas spirit. But Marie and I soon had them smiling. One soldier told me that he was surprised that we would take time out from our holiday celebrations to visit them. We brought pastries and sweets for the men and we all went from room to room singing Russian carols.

I realized today that I have so much to be thankful for, Nina. I've been feeling very sorry for myself lately and forget how many wonderful people and things I have in my life.

2 January 1917

Dear Nina,

Rumors have reached the palace that there is increasing unrest in Russia among the common people. They think that Mama is ruling the country while Papa is away at war and they resent that. Mama is not Russian and many of the people have always resented the fact that Papa chose her to be Tsarina, instead of a Russian princess.

Poor Mama. It has always been difficult for her. She has never felt that she was a part of this country and she knows that most of the people hate her. It is one of the reasons that we have remained somewhat secluded here in the palace, attending functions only when absolutely necessary.

These ceremonies that we must attend are awfully boring. And we must sit stone-still for hours. I've always admired Mama's way of remaining in one place for hours without even a twitch. One day, after a particularly lengthy ceremony during which I was scolded several times for fidgeting, I asked Mama how she stayed so still for such a long time.

"I pray," she said.

I even fidget after a few minutes of praying!

5 January 1917

Oh Nina,

Papa has told Mama that he wants Alexis to stay with him at the Front. He is to learn the art of ruling and soldiering. Monsieur Gilliard will accompany Alexis to Mohilof and will remain there in order to tutor him.

Mama is very upset but she must abide by Papa's wishes in this matter. Alexis is the only one who is happy to be going. I certainly am not. I will miss my little brother.

First the war takes my father, now my brother!

8 January 1917

Alexis left this morning with Monsieur Gilliard. We all cried so many tears but Mama has been crying all day. It was difficult to concentrate on our lessons with Mme Schneider and I was scolded twice for looking out the window, Nina, but I don't care. It was not a good day for any of us.

10 January 1917

We all went to Mass this morning, Nina, before going to the hospital. I fidget more than I pray, but I am able to get some prayers in during time in church. Father Vasileff says that God knows our prayers before we ask them. If that is so, then why must we pray so hard and long before our prayers are answered?

I pray for Papa and Alexis that they return home soon. We all miss Alexis; the palace is not quite the same without him.

13 January 1917

Oh, Nina,

I saw Gleb today!!!

We have all been so unhappy since Alexis and Papa left, that our mood must have touched Mama. She told us this morning that she had a surprise for us after our lessons. The surprise was that she invited Gleb and his sister, Tatiana, to join us for our walk in the park today!

Gleb looked so-o-o handsome. I found that I was very shy around him. I had never felt that way before. But then, I wasn't in love with him the last time I saw him. I suppose that makes a difference.

Gleb was very friendly to all of us and did not single me out for special attention. This disappointed me, but of course he couldn't very well show his true feelings in front of everyone.

It was so wonderful to be able to talk to our old friends and share some of our worries with them. They already knew about Papa and Alexis because their father keeps them informed about the goings-on in the palace. They were most sympathetic towards us.

Gleb had his sketch pad with him and we played a game that we used to play when we were together in Livadia for the summer. Gleb draws caricatures of people at court and Marie and I create a story about them. The pictures were very funny and we really tried to make the dialogue just as comical. What fun we all had! It was wonderful to laugh and run together and remember old times. And, Nina, Gleb didn't call me "little Duchess" even once.

When we returned to the palace, we thanked Mama for our surprise and we begged her to let Gleb and Tatiana visit more often. "I promise to consider it," she said. Mama always says that same thing when she doesn't want to commit herself to a firm resolve.

17 January 1917

We have received terrible news today, Nina. Mama was awakened by one of the servants who delivered a telegram from Papa, "Alexis very ill. Returning home immediately."

We are preparing to meet Papa's train when it arrives at Petersburg this evening.

Mama has been walking around the palace crying and wringing her hands. We are all sick with the worry of not knowing what is happening to poor Alexis.

18 January 1917

Dear Nina,

What a state the palace was in last evening when we all arrived home from the train station with Alexis and Papa. All the servants were bustling about, carrying luggage, putting on pots of tea, preparing food for Papa. And poor dear Alexis. How pale he looked. How near death!

It seems that Alexis had a cold, and one time he sneezed so hard that he burst a blood vessel in his nose. This caused him to bleed and of course, he couldn't stop bleeding. The military doctor was able to help Alexis a little, but he recommended that Papa return to Tsarkoe Selo as soon as possible.

Lessons resume as usual no matter what catastrophe takes place here. Mama feels that without our routine, we will just spend our time worrying and fretting about Alexis, when there is nothing to be done. During my lessons, I whispered small prayers to God that he heal our little brother.

19 January 1917

Listen to this, Nina!

Olga heard some rumors from Cook's kitchen today. Cook and the servants were talking about an argument that Mama and Papa had about Alexis. Mama said that Alexis will never return to the Front again and Papa got very angry.

"Our son is the future ruler of Russia. How can he learn what is necessary if he is always at home with his mother?"

Mama was very insistent. I'm sure that this time she will get her way.

21 January 1917

Dear Nina,

I think that Papa should do more for the poor people in Russia. We have so much money and so many fine things and there are so many who do not have anything, especially since the war started. Even bread has been scarce and there are people who are going to bed hungry every night. Sometimes I am ashamed to live in this palace with all this luxury. It doesn't seem fair.

25 January 1917

Papa left for the Front again this morning. He told us that he was needed there and now that Alexis is out of danger, he must leave.

I understand that Papa's soldiers need him, but does Papa know that we also need him?

1 February 1917

Oh Nina,

I am so worried! A revolt has started!

Olga happened to come upon three of the servants talking in excited whispers. She said that they stopped when they saw her, and when she demanded to know what was happening to stir them up, they did not want to tell her.

"Your Highness, the Empress would be very upset with us if she knew that we were worrying you with our gossip."

"I feel that something is terribly wrong," Olga said. "and I command you to tell me what you were talking about so anxiously."

Then they told her that there were several riots in Petrograd last night. The people, the servants said, are distraught. Since Papa will not change things, they feel that they must make the changes themselves.

I know that they are wrong. Papa is trying to do the best he can. He is so busy planning and fighting the war that he can't take care of things in Russia too. The people must have patience and trust that when the war is over, Papa will address their needs.

Later: I asked Monsieur Gilliard about the riots. I wanted to know his opinion on the political situation. Monsieur said that this was the start of a revolution by the people who were trying to make a statement – a plea to Papa to do something to help them. Monsieur doesn't think that there is anything to be concerned about.

"I doubt that you will hear about any more riots. Besides, we are safe here at the palace and if anyone tries to hurt us, the Royal Guard will be here to protect us."

I pray that Monsieur Gilliard is right.

5 February 1917

Dear Nina,

Papa is home again!

Light snow fell during the night, which isn't remarkable in any way since it is always snowing in Russia during the winter. But, it is bitter cold. I heard Elise, one of the chamber maids, tell Mama that it is several degrees below zero.

So we stayed indoors all day. We weren't even allowed to visit at the hospital. After our lessons were over for the day, Mama decided that our confinement should be spent in a fruitful way. She suggested to Tatiana and Olga that they spend the morning preparing bandages for the hospital, which she delivered in the afternoon when it became a little warmer. Marie and I had to complete the needlework that we had started many months ago.

I do detest needlework only because I must sit still for a long time. Tatiana says that I will make a terrible wife. She says that I am not good at any of the feminine arts and that no one will want to marry me. She also says that Mama will have to pay someone to be my husband.

Oh, how furious she makes me sometimes! Tatiana thinks she is so wonderful, but I know that Mama will have to beg a man to marry HER!

9 February 1917

Papa is leaving us again, Nina. Mama wants him to stay here with us. She is afraid that the riots will reach Tsarskoe Selo and the palace. Papa tried to allay her fears by reminding her that the Royal Guard is here to protect us.

"I trust them completely. They will protect you and the children and I will keep abreast of what is happening here. If the situation worsens, I promise to return home immediately."

Papa seems to feel that it is imperative that he be with his men at the Front. Nina, sometimes I think that Papa cares more about his soldiers than he does about us.

16 February 1917

Nina,

Aunt Elizabeth visited with us today. Mama was so happy to see her sister that she nearly cried when it was announced that she had arrived at the palace.

Aunt Elizabeth is a nun. Some years ago she founded a religious community in Germany and she is now the head of about twenty women who devote their life to God. They spend their entire day in prayer and doing good works of charity. Aunt Elizabeth is a very holy woman.

We were all invited to tea in Mama's sitting room. Aunt Elizabeth said that she had to return in two days. She told Mama that God sent her a message tell her to visit the palace immediately. She started to speak of the unrest that is taking place outside of the palace, when Mama stopped her.

"Elizabeth, perhaps we should discuss this later. The girls must return to their lessons, and I'm sure they would like to talk to you in the brief time which they have."

I know that it is Mama's way of hiding things from us. She doesn't want us to worry or be afraid. If she knew that we have been privy to information through the kitchen and the servants, she would be very upset.

21 February 1917

Oh Nina,

There were more riots in Petrograd this morning. The supply of bread ran out and the bake shops didn't open. After waiting on line for hours, people became angry smashing windows and stealing whatever food they could find.

When we asked Monsieur Gilliard about these rumors, he explained that most of the food is being sent to the men fighting in the war. The little food that is still left in the city is so highly priced that the people cannot afford to purchase it on the poor wages they earn. Black bread is the only item that they can afford to buy and now that all the bread is gone, they will not have any food to give to their families.

It doesn't seem fair that we in the palace have so much to eat and there may be children in Petrograd without any food. I asked Mama if we could send some of our food to the people.

"That is a generous thought, Ana," she replied. "However, we have so many mouths to feed here in the palace that if we give away our food, the people here would starve."

She also said that there were hundreds of thousands of peasants and working people and we could not possibly feed all of them. How SAD!!

26 February 1917

Nina, Alexis is very ill and Mama is distraught with worry. His face is covered with red spots; Dr. Botkin says that he has a disease called measles and although he will feel sick for awhile, he will not likely die from it.

I peeked in to visit Alexis today while Mama was visiting the hospital. She would be furious with me if she knew. She gave firm orders that we were not to go near Alexis while he was ill. But I just had to see him and hold his hand.

1 March 1917

Now, I've got the measles, Nina! Dr. Botkin told Mama that we might all succumb to the disease and he was correct. I have been in bed for the last two days. I suppose I should have listened to Mama and not visited Alexis the other day. I am really too sick to write very much but wanted to tell you about my illness.

5 March 1917

Nina,

This is the first day I've been able to get out of my sickbed. Doctor Botkin gave permission for me to sit in a chair near the window with a warm rug over my lap. He said that in a couple of days I'll be my "very happy self again".

I've only eaten broth, tea, and toast for days but I suppose it's more than those poor people in Petrograd are getting to eat. My appetite is slowly returning though, and I want Cook to make some of my favorite foods.

I've made an inspection of my face this morning and was relieved to see that most of my spots have disappeared. My face shows less roundness than usual which I suppose is due to the meager diet I've been on.

I'm still very weak, Nina, and must end my writing for the day.

6 March 1917

Dear Nina,

Alexis visited me this morning against Mama's orders; she is afraid that he will become ill again.

Mama came in just after Alexis left my room. Tatiana and Olga now have the measles also, and it's my entire fault for disobeying Mama's orders and visiting Alexis that day. As soon as they are well, I'll confess my part in this and tell them how sorry I am that I made them ill. Only Marie hasn't become sick. Doctor Botkin said that he doubts that she will. He said that she has a "strong constitution", whatever that means.

8 March 1917

Dearest Nina,

Marie had a nightmare last night in which peasants stormed
the palace and took Mama and Alexis away. She said that she
tried to run after them but they kept getting further into the
distance and she knew that she'd never see them again.

Marie was crying while telling us about her dream. I
started crying too. All the fear that I've been holding in all
day just burst into sobs.

13 March 1917

Nina,

I'm so scared!

Mama came into our room this morning. She told us that the situation outside the palace is becoming dangerous. She told us that we must remain calm and not worry too much because an army of soldiers is going to arrive soon to help the Royal Guard protect the palace. Mama also sent a wire to Papa telling him of our situation and begging him to come home to help us.

Riots are taking place everywhere and there is even talk of storming the palace and taking Mama and Alexis as prisoners. (You can be sure Mama didn't give us this information. We learned about this through our usual sources.) This is very scary because it echoes Marie's dream of the other night. Could her dream be a forewarning of something to come?

I can hardly concentrate on my lessons without thinking of what might happen and there is a feeling of panic in my stomach. We received a message from Papa that he will be leaving Mohileff as soon as possible. He reminded us that we are safe in the palace and must remain calm until he arrives.

Later: I think that I will always remember the events of this afternoon no matter how long I live.

After tea today, Mama called all of us, except Alexis, into her drawing room. She told us that she had something very difficult to tell us but that we must all be brave and calm. Mama said that Papa has given up his throne and his rule of Russia. Olga told me later that this is called 'abdication'. Mama said that Alexis is really the next heir to the throne, but Papa felt that since Alexis is so ill all the time, the throne should be given to a stronger ruler. She then told us that Papa gave up his rule to Uncle Michael, his brother, but then Uncle Michael turned the rule over to a new form of government called the Duma.

Mama could hardly speak by the time she finished giving us the news. We all cried and hugged each other but Mama cried the hardest. Then she said, "My dear daughters, you must remember something. Although the Russian people no longer thank of Papa and myself as their rulers, you are still princesses and your father and I are still Tsar and Tsarina. We all have the blood of royalty and that is something that no one, not even the Russian people, can take away from us."

17 March 1917

Dear Nina,

Papa's soldiers surround the entire palace and we are all very excited. I feel very safe now and can't understand why Mama still looks so worried.

Last night, Tatiana, Olga and I ran from room to room looking out at the campfires the soldiers had built around the palace. From whatever window we looked, we could see armed guards. Marie doesn't share in our excitement. She is very fearful and nervous about what could happen. I told her that no one can get past the soldiers and their weapons, although I do hope that no one tries. I don't want them to kill anyone in trying to save us.

Papa has not yet returned, so Mama felt it was her place to talk to the soldiers as he would have done. Marie begged to accompany her while the rest of us watched from the window. She and Mama bundled into their heaviest coats and left the palace for the first time in days, to talk to the guards. Marie later told us that Mama was shown great respect by the men as she went to each one of them and expressed her thanks for keeping us safe.

When Mama and Marie came inside, we ran to hug them. Their cheeks were wet with tears and we cried also. Mama said that Papa would he here soon and then everything would be alright.

I don't think Mama really believes that. I think she is very scared and is trying to put on a brave face for us.

21 March 1917

Monsieur Gilliard told us this morning that when Papa was saying good-bye to his staff at the Front, several of the officers burst into tears. He said that there are many in the army who want Papa to continue to be Commander-in-Chief of the army. But too many others want him to leave.

29 March 1917

Marie is very ill, Nina. She had the vapors this morning and couldn't get out of bed. Mama asked if she was having her monthlies, but she said no, so Mama sent for Doctor Botkin. After examining Marie, he told Mama that she has pneumonia and must be kept in bed for many days.

Mama thinks she got a chill when she went outside the other night to greet the soldiers. We are all praying for her to get better.

5 April 1917

Dear Nina,

Mama has received some terrible news but she won't tell us what it is about. She will only tell us that Papa is well and that he will be home soon. But Mama is not well. Her face is wet with tears and she looks quite pale. I cannot imagine what news could devastate her so much, if Papa is alive and well.

We haven't been outside of the palace in weeks. Mama says that it isn't safe. The time for our studies has been increased by Madame Schneider, and Monsieur Gilliard is devoting almost as much time to us girls as he usually gives to Alexis. I think that Mama has told both of them to keep us occupied so we will have less time to worry.

Marie has been getting better each day. She was able to get out of bed today for the first time.

6 April 1917

The soldiers have deserted us, Nina!!

They have joined the revolutionaries who want us out of the country. That is the news that upset Mama yesterday. In place of Papa's Royal Guard, new soldiers have arrived, but they are not here to protect us, but to guard us from escaping the palace, until the new government decides what to do with us. A summons was given that anyone who wanted to leave the palace (meaning the servants), must do so before 4 o'clock today or they will become prisoners along with my family. We are all so SCARED! And where is Papa? Will they let him come into the palace when he arrives?

Later:

Most of the servants have left, but those closest to us stayed on. The doors of the palace are now locked and no one is permitted to leave or enter. I now fear more than ever for Papa's safety in his travels, yet I also fear for his safety when he reaches the palace.

Mama is keeping us busy with needlework and studies. She is trying to keep a normalcy to our day and insists that we go about our day as if nothing unusual is taking place. Everyone about the palace seems strained and it is difficult not to notice.

I think Alexis is taking the news of Papa's abdication the hardest. He doesn't understand why Papa did what he did, but I told him that we must trust that Papa did the right thing for all of us and for Russia as well.

11 April 1917

Nina,

Papa has finally come home. It was Tatiana who saw him first. She was looking out the window of her room when she saw a car stop in front of the palace. She said that she just knew that it was Papa, and it was. We all ran into his arms the second he walked in the door and we hugged him while we cried. Alexis was in his room when Papa arrived and after greeting us, Papa flew up the stairs two at a time to see him and Mama. I do feel safer now that Papa is here to take care of us.

We took luncheon together today as a celebration of Papa's arrival. Mama looked happier than I've seen her in a long time but she didn't have much to say. Papa, however, looks very pale and tired. I'm sure that being at the Front is a terribly unpleasant affair and Papa is just worn out by it all.

I did make him laugh though. I told him the story of how Madame Borokof came to see Mama one day a few weeks ago. Madame was wearing a feather in her hat. When she bent over to kiss Mama's hand, the feather touched Mama's nose and tickled it, which made her sneeze. Everyone in the room laughed except Mama and Madame, who was very embarrassed.

Papa thought my story was very funny and he laughed heartily. I felt very proud when he said to me, "Ana, no one can make me laugh as much as you can. It is a gift which I hope you will always treasure."

15 April 1917

Happy Easter, Nina!

It is Easter Sunday today, the celebration of the resurrection of our Lord after he was murdered by his enemies because they were afraid of him. I am sure that many Russians would like to kill all of us out of fear that we will keep them hungry and poor while we lavish riches on ourselves. This is just not true. We did not steal this palace and all the riches it holds from the people, it was passed down to Papa as the ruler of Russia. It has been in our family for three hundred years. Certainly we cannot be faulted for that!

Mama said that this should be my special day because my name also signifies the resurrection. Anastasia means 'she who will rise again'.

"A name is never given without help from a Higher Source, Ana. Your name was whispered into my heart when you were born and perhaps someday you will know why the Lord chose you to receive this name."

Sadly enough, we could no longer go to our beautiful church, Fyodorvsky Cathedral for the Easter services. Instead, services will be held in the chapel right here in the palace.

17 April 1917

Dearest Nina,

The guards still surround the palace but Papa told us not to pay any attention to them. We are kept very busy with our studies and Monsieur Gilliard sees to it that we have lots of writing to do. I barely have time to write to you, Nina, and sometimes must sneak a candle and write in a corner of our bedroom while Marie sleeps.

Papa spends a good deal of time in his office. I heard him tell Mama that he is not allowed to walk in the park but must confine his daily strolls to our small garden. Papa doesn't seem to mind it. Once the temperature warms, we will also be able to walk in the garden because it is guarded by a soldier with a rifle. But as far as going to the hospital, that is over.

20 April 1917

Nina,

There is talk that we will be made to leave Russia and go to England. Mama wants us to all be well so we are able to travel when the time comes.

England is so rainy and damp all the time, and where would we live? Would our English relatives give us a palace to live in or would we have to maintain a small house? My English cousins are so boring; I would hate to have to live with them!

21 April 1917

I HATE the Russian people, Nina. Papa has done so much for them and this is the manner in which they repay him. At this moment, I am not proud to be a Russian.

22 April 1917

Nina,

We all went to chapel this morning to give thanks for Papa's safe return home. The priest has to come here since we are not allowed to leave, even to go to church.

Marie is ill again. Doctor Botkin said that she must not leave her room for a couple of days. He has moved into the palace, since the guards will not let him come and go as he pleases.

I suggested to Mama that I might stay and keep Marie company, but I think she saw through my plan. Mama was insistent that I attend the services. She said that it is the first time that we will be in chapel as a family since Papa has come home and that I MUST be there.

We had to get permission from Colonel Kerensky who is in charge of the guards. He sent a message that it would be allowed only if we had a guard of at least ten soldiers with us. He is so afraid that we will escape.

Where can we go? We are so far away from any form of transportation and it would be impossible for us to get through St. Petersburg without being recognized. I don't think he needs to trouble himself so much.

I always fidget in chapel and Mama is always sending me looks to be still. I want to get up and move about and I can't tolerate sitting still for more than a few minutes.

Today, Father Doborkny said a special prayer that Russia would be successful in the war and that we would all be protected from harm. It was at this moment that Mama started to cry. I don't think anyone else noticed but I could see that her face was wet with tears.

27 April 1917

Colonel Kerensky came to the palace today, Nina. We were all in Tatiana and Olga's room. Mama was reading us a tale from the "Arabian Nights". I was so concentrated on Mama's voice and the events of the story that I jumped when the door flew open and a strange man burst into the room. None of us knew who he was until he introduced himself and Mama was very upset that he should enter our rooms unannounced.

"Colonel Kerensky," she said. "Perhaps you are unaware that one does not enter the private rooms of the Grand Duchesses without being announced."

"Alexandra Romanov," he replied. "Perhaps you are unaware that you are not longer the Tsarina and this palace now belongs to the people of Russia. It is I who can come and go as I please, not you."

We all looked at Mama whose face turned very red. I've never seen her look so angry.

"Very well, Colonel," she replied. "Since you are here, what is it that you wish?"

"I will meet with you and your husband immediately. I will escort you myself."

Mama handed the book to Olga and asked her to finish reading. Then she followed the Colonel out the door.

It was a few minutes before we could speak. We had never heard anyone address Mama by any other title except Tsarina or Your Highness. Also, no one had ever been so bold as to give Mama an order. It is she who commands others.

Olga started to read but she had to stop because she was unable to see through her tears. We all started crying then. I think we cried for Mama but perhaps we cried a little for ourselves and for a way of life that is being snatched from us.

28 April 1917

Oh, Nina

Why is all of this happening? Have I been so bad that I and my family must be punished? We have become prisoners in our own home. I sometimes pray that I will realize that I am dreaming all of this, that I will awaken and everything will be as it was before.

Nina, I'm so glad I can tell you all of these things. I feel as if I'd burst if I wasn't able to share with anyone.

4 May 1917

Papa has been separated from us again! He is still in the palace but he is being kept a prisoner in another part of the building. Monsieur Gilliard came to our apartments this morning and told us.

It seems as if all of Russia hates Papa. I don't understand why people would dislike a man who is nothing but sweet and gentle and who loves his country so much.

Olga said that Doctor Botkin told her that the Russian people blame Papa and grandfather and all the past rulers of Russia for their problems. He said that the people don't want a Tsar and Tsarina to tell them what to do anymore. They want the common people to make the laws and rules. I don't think anyone but a Tsar or a King can rule a country as big as Russia.

The weather is getting nicer but we are not allowed to go outside. I've taken some pictures of the guards outside the palace but I am on my last roll of film. Marie said that I shouldn't waste my precious film taking pictures of the soldiers, but I don't think it's a waste. Someday, I will be able to show them to my children and tell them stories about what it was like to be a prisoner in our own palace.

10 May 1917

Everyone is quite glum now, Nina. I can't seem to make anyone laugh anymore. Olga and Marie are the gloomiest and they walk around with a long face all day. They say that there is great cause for worry and if I ignore it I am just being a fool. So, I guess I must begin to wear a long face just like the rest of them. It's very boring being that way. I'd rather remember the happy times we had. I am sure that these times will come again especially if we are sent to England. Mama says that there are people who are trying to help us but she doesn't know when it will happen.

"You must pray constantly to our Lord and to our Good Friend in heaven that we will soon be able to leave the palace and begin a new life in England," she told us.

I try to remember to pray, but I forget. Sometimes, I start to pray when I go to bed, but I always fall asleep before the last words form in my mind.

14 May 1917

Dear Nina,

Our days seem to be conducted as usual but there are certain things that we are not allowed to have or do. Most of all, I miss not being able to visit with Gleb. I still hide his picture under my pillow at night. Then, during the day, I give it to your safe-keeping, Nina.

While we were having our tea tonight, Olga mentioned that the thing she missed the most was not having any fruit. She is very conscious of her diet and she knows that fruit is very important for a healthy body.

Colonel Kerensky stopped all deliveries of fresh fruit to us, saying that it was a luxury that we did not deserve. Marie said that the thing she misses most is our visits to the hospital. Fresh flowers are the things that Tatiana and Mama miss the most. The plants in our greenhouse have all died because no one was permitted to go there and water them. The palace seems empty without fresh flowers in every room. And of course, we all miss Papa since he has been held a prisoner in a different part of the palace.

19 May 1917

I'm frightened, Nina! The situation here has become worse as the days have passed. Alexis is very ill again. Yesterday, he bumped his leg while playing with me and Marie and he has been confined to his bed ever since. Doctor Botkin is with him almost all the time and Mama, too. Papa is permitted to join Mama for evening tea but a soldier is always present so they can say very little to each other in privacy. They are forbidden to speak in anything but Russian. Mama told us that Papa is well and sends his love to us all. He had asked permission to visit Alexis, but Colonel Kerensky refused his request.

Except for the few servants that have remained with us, we see no one else, nor do we receive letters from the outside. We are not allowed to use the telephone, which doesn't bother us a bit, but I know Mama misses it. We are being made to go on with our studies as if all were normal. I would like to suggest to Colonel Kerensky that Mme. Schneider be sent away. I would be very happy about that.

And, Nina, Doctor Botkin told me that Gleb had written a letter to me and gave it to his father to deliver. But Doctor Botkin refused to carry it as he is searched thoroughly before entering and leaving the palace. He is afraid that if we disobey Colonel Kerensky's rules, it will become worse for us and we will suffer even more than we do now.

He did try to write to me, Nina! I'm so happy just knowing that.

23 May 1917

The palace has become so foreign to us that we hardly recognize it as our home anymore. All paintings, art work, silver, table settings; indeed anything of value has been confiscated by the new government. We dine on tableware of the plainest quality. It is, in fact, the same dishes and utensils that our servants used in the kitchen.

Papa's Imperial train has also been seized, along with the Standart and the Imperial car. In fact, it was in Papa's car that Colonel Kerensky arrived at the palace the other day, and the car was driven by one of Papa's chauffeurs!

The only rooms that have remained almost unchanged are our bedrooms. Mama's sitting room did not escape the plunder since it had been decorated very grandly with paintings and valuable pieces from England. Mama was very upset when the palace ruffians descended upon her room, but she had to sit quietly while they searched and stripped it of all but the barest necessities.

Poor Papa has had to give up his wonderful study to Colonel Kerensky who also stripped the room of any décor and transformed it into a cold, barren space. It now resembles the room of a monk rather than that which once belonged to the Emperor of Russia.

But we must bear all of this, Nina. We are unable to fight back, which makes us feel powerless and frustrated. I am sure that we will never again behold our possessions. We will be reduced to the simplest of circumstances.

29 May 1917

Dear Nina,

We walked in the park today. The weather was so beautiful. Of course, the guards walked with us, always close to us, never at a discreet distance. They must always be privy to every word that we speak between ourselves.

31 May 1917

Nina,

The palace garden is quite large and a portion of the garden has been set aside for us to use. A key to the garden gate is kept by the Commandant of the Guard, and we can only walk during fixed hours.

Today, there were citizens outside the gates of the park watching us, staring with dislike and contempt. They called out in a foul language to Papa. They yelled horrible things at my mother. I heard the name Rasputin linked with the name of my mother and I couldn't bear anymore. I held my hands over my ears and tried to walk faster. I'm sure that only the presence of the guards insured our safety, as the people were angry enough to storm the gates and hurt all of us.

They hate my father, these people. They think that he is responsible for all of Russia's miseries, but it's not the truth. Papa would give his life for Russia and for the Russian people. Is there no one in Russia who cares about Papa?

6 June 1917

Nina,

Last night, I dreamt that we were on the Standart heading towards Livadia. Olga and I stood on the deck watching the seagulls in formation overhead. I could feel the heat from the sun warming my face, which a moment before had felt ice cold. Suddenly, the water was filled with soldiers. Olga and I stood in terror as the soldiers came on board the Standart. I screamed and tried to run but my legs were still and they wouldn't move.

My own screams awoke me and everyone else, too. Mama rushed into our room thinking that one of the soldiers had invaded our bedroom. When I told her about my dream, Mama said that she was not surprised that I would have such a dream. There were soldiers everywhere and we can hardly make a move without them. Colonel Kerensky says that the soldiers are maintained to protect us but we know that he's lying. We are prisoners in our own home!

7 June 1917

Dear Nina,

My spirits were lifted today. The sun was warm and a soft breeze was blowing my hair around. We were given permission to walk again today, which came as a surprise to all of us. Colonel Kerensky is usually not so generous.

I didn't want to go out for fear that people were again standing outside the gates and I would have to hear their insults and blasphemies. But Tatiana urged me to go.

"Those people cannot hurt us. They can only express what they think and just because they think it doesn't make it true."

She is right, of course. Papa came with us for our walk and Mama followed in her wheelchair. I soon forgot how concerned I was because the day was so beautiful. Summer has finally come to Tsarkoe Selo.

Yesterday at Mass, Father Duborkny talked about life and death and its relationship to the seasons. He said that winter signifies the death of all of nature but it is to be reborn again when spring comes. He did not say that of humans; however, Mama says that we are born only once and then we return to our heavenly home.

It makes me wonder why I must learn so much in this life, only to lose it when I die. Hundreds of hours spent at the piano and at my studies; it seems almost futile if tomorrow, or next year, I died. A lot of people do not live very long lives. To what purpose were they born when they are only allowed to live for a few years or a few hours?

I once read in a book that people in the country of India believe that they live many lives; they are born over and over again. In one life they may be a farmer, in another life a husband, in another a wife, in another a king or queen. This seems to make more sense to me.

Mama would be upset if she knew what I was thinking. But I share my thoughts with you, dear Nina.

12 June 1917

Good news, Nina!

Colonel Kerensky gave us permission this afternoon, to start a little vegetable garden in a corner of the park. It is a small patch but large enough to grow several varieties of vegetables.

Mama had stored seeds in a jar in her sitting room and Tatiana ran to fetch them. We used these to start seedlings which we will plant in the ground as soon as they have grown a few inches high. Tatiana, Marie, Olga and I planted the seeds in small pots while Papa, Monsieur Gilliard, and Doctor Botkin dug up the plot. At the end of the two hours we were all tired but happier than we had been in a long time.

14 June 1917

Happy Summer! Nina

It's a beautiful day! The air is warm and even hot when I
stand in the sun. The flowers from last year's seeds are fully
grown now. I feel peaceful and happy today and a renewed
sense of hopefulness has captured my heart.

Colonel Kobylinsky is the new Commander of the
Revolutionary Guard. He has replaced Colonel Kerensky.
The new commander introduced himself to Mama and Papa
this morning. He is much nicer than Colonel Kerensky and
treats us with more respect than anyone else. It is the Colonel
who gave us permission to walk outdoors two hours each day,
a privilege that we were denied before; we were limited to
about 30 minutes. What a wonderful gift!

18 June 1917

Dear Nina,

Today is my sixteenth birthday! It's not a very happy day for me though. Everyone gave me presents that they had made, and Mama gave me another diamond to add to my collection as she's done each year since I was born. This should have been a special birthday for me but it's not. If circumstances were different, I would be attending a magnificent party here at the palace and all my diamonds would be made into a necklace which I would show off at the ball, and I would be the center of attention. But none of this will happen because our lives are not the same. I hate my life!

19 June 1917

Poor Papa! It seems that when Colonel Kobylinsky is not here, the soldiers feel that they can be as disrespectful to us as they please. Today, Papa was riding his bicycle through the park and as he passed a couple of soldiers, one of them pushed the bayonet from his rifle into the spokes of the bicycle wheel. Papa fell to the ground and since it had rained during the night, he was covered with mud and dirt. As we ran over to help Papa, we could hear the soldiers laughing at him.

I've never been so angry, Nina. Even when my cousin Felix stole and ate my box of chocolates, I was angry but never angrier than I was today. For the first time in my whole life I wished that I were a strong man, a soldier, so that I could defend Papa. Papa is in his forty-ninth year, an old man, and cannot defend himself. But what can a sixteen year old do, especially when she is a girl? Nothing.

26 June 1917

Dear Nina,

Life goes on as usual here. Monsieur Gilliard says that humans are very adaptable creatures and I think we have all done very well in adapting to our new life in the palace.

We still rise at about eight o'clock and take breakfast in our rooms. It usually consists of tea and a bowl of grains. Sugar and flour are now considered extravagances and are not allowed here at the palace. Therefore, Cook can no longer bake her little breakfast treats for us as she used to do, and I sometimes long for them with all my heart.

We are not longer allowed to bathe every day, something which I am grateful for, so we must take turns washing in the basin. On the days when we are given permission to have a bath, we spend a good part of our mornings doing this. Mama insists that we continue our piano playing and needlepoint, so the rest of the morning is given to these activities.

After lunch, which usually includes cabbage, potatoes, and a small slice of bread, Monsieur Gilliard begins our lessons. He is now our only tutor since Mme. Schneider left with many of the household staff the day before we were put under arrest. I really don't miss her, Nina. She was terribly prim and proper and I really prefer Monsieur Gilliard. I've never enjoyed lessons and I don't enjoy them now, however, when Monsieur is here, I don't think about what is happening around us. He keeps us busy for hours with school work and practice.

In the late afternoon, we take our two-hour walk in the park or we tend to the garden. I feel very comfortable as long as there are no onlookers present. However, on those days when people are lined up at the fence, we cut short our walk. I think it's better to be indoors during these times, than outside where

95

the air is filled with hatred and anger.

In the evening we work on the lessons that Monsieur has assigned and then we can do as we please until it is time to go to bed. Colonel Kobylinsky insists that all lights in the palace must be out at ten o'clock, so even Mama and Papa must retire at that hour.

On the surface, our life doesn't seem so different than we have been used to, but it is actually very strange. We don't have the freedom to do as we please within our own home, we are prohibited from working in the hospital, our food rations get cut weekly, we can't have any contact with the outside world, and we live in fear of not knowing what will become of us.

5 July 1917

Our garden seems to be the focus of our day now. All of us, including Monsieur Gilliard and Doctor Botkin, look forward to tending our small plot of land. I was the first to spot new seedlings today, and in about a week, they should be strong enough to go in the ground. By the end of the summer, we can eat the fruits of our labor – cabbages, lettuce, tomatoes and other vegetables. These will help add to our food rations which have been getting smaller each week.

The only difficulty in tending the garden is in getting enough water to the seedlings. Monsieur Gilliard thought of the idea that we should use a large wash tub, which we found near the servants quarters. We take turns carrying the tub into the kitchen for water and then dragging it back outside to the garden. Sometimes, the guards help us but usually it takes two of us to drag the heavy tub into the yard. Then, with the aid of cups and our hands, when other implements aren't available, we throw water over the plants, making sure that all the ground is saturated with water.

I find it interesting that this task, under different circumstances could be tedious, but now it has become fun. We all laugh and have a great time. Also, we're working for the good of us all.

11 July 1917

I took photographs today of everyone in the park. Monsieur Gilliard told me that I must stand with my back to the sun or else the light will ruin my picture. So, I have learned something new about taking pictures.

Doctor Botkin gave me a drawing from Gleb. He said that he found it between the pages of his medical manuals. It as a sketch of a bear (Papa) skating with his family (us) here on the pond at Tsarkoe Selo. Everyone laughed when I showed them the drawing because Gleb had depicted a likeness of each one of us on the bodies of bears.

I haven't forgotten about Gleb. I just don't think it does me any good to give my heart to a man right now, when I don't know where we will be tomorrow.

15 July 1917

Dear Nina,

Today when I was walking in the park, I was daydreaming about things we used to do BR (Before the Revolution). I was remembering the times Mama took us to England to visit her relatives there. We were treated with the same reverence and respect which we used to receive at home in Russia.

The English seem to have a deep devotion to their royal family. I remember that it was a thrill for me to sit still in the royal box at the theatre, which we attended on each visit.

And, Nina, I remember our trips to the Crimea each fall. These were gloriously long trips on the Standart where we could stand on deck and watch as we passed the small villages. Captain Derevenko always slowed the boat down when we were passing a village because the Turkish villages were so pretty to look at with their whitewashed stone houses. The gardens were filled with fruits and flowers of infinite varieties. Every village had its own church which towered above the village houses.

Sometimes, we would stop the Standart and row to shore in order to climb the hills and mountains. These were filled with patches of strawberries which grew there until December. When we had filled our bellies and baskets with strawberries, we would head to the grape arbors which lined every road to the village. I often returned to the boat sick to my stomach after eating as much of these delicious fruits as I could get my hands on.

Oh Nina, will my life ever be the same again? Will we ever go to Livadia again? Sometimes I just want to cry over the unfairness of this!

21 July 1917

Yesterday during our walk, the gate was lined with soldiers and peasants, all of them trying to get a look at us. We had only been outside for a few minutes when someone started saying nasty words to Mama and Papa. Then others followed with insults and rude remarks. A guard finally urged us to go indoors because he was afraid that we might be in danger. I wanted to tell him that he should be making the peasants go away and let us enjoy the little outdoor time that we have. But I can't say a word. It's so FRUSTRATING!

29 July 1917

Olga overheard Monsieur Gilliard and Mama talking. The government has decided to move us out of the palace. But we don't know where or when. Oh, Nina, this not knowing what will happen to us is terrible!

4 August 1917

We all went swimming in the pond today, including Alexis. It was great fun and for a short time we forgot all our troubles. I forgot the soldiers and the revolution and everything, Nina. It was so wonderful to take a break from worry! But as soon as we returned to the palace, the fear in my stomach started up again. I want it to go away. I want never to be scared again!

12 August 1917

Dearest Nina,

Today is Alexis's 13th birthday! He's not feeling very well so we all took turns in his room, hugging him and giving him presents. We all love him so much!

Olga, Tatiana, Marie and I gave Alexis a sweater that we took turns knitting for him. We also made him a special birthday card and signed it "OTMA" our new signature. (Each of the letters stands for the first letter of our names.) Sadly, though, there will be no celebration tonight at dinner.

Later: Mama came into our rooms today while Monsieur was giving a history lesson. At first, I was relieved to see Mama's figure in the doorway because I was practically bored to tears, but on look on her face told me that something very serious had happened. My first thought was that Colonel Kobylinsky had decided to send Papa away from us but, in fact, Mama told us that we are all leaving tomorrow night for an unknown destination. She said that the provisional government feels that it is too dangerous for us to remain in the palace much longer. It seems that the Revolution is getting worse and most of the grievances of the people are directed at us. Colonel Kobylinsky has been ordered to move us to a safer place but he will not tell Mama or Papa where we are going.

Mama confessed that she had hoped it would be Livadia, but when Colonel Kobylinsky told her that we were to bring warm clothing and heavy coats, she was certain our destination was elsewhere. We are to pack the things we want to take with us and be ready to leave tomorrow evening. Don't worry, Nina, I'm taking you with me.

13 August 1917

Dear Nina,

We have all been very busy getting ready to leave. In a way, I'm not too sorry to leave the palace because it has not been our home for a long time now. Mama has instructed us to pack as little as possible but she said that we must include at least three books with our belongings. I have decided to bring "Great Expectations" by Charles Dickens and "Tale of Two Cities". I'm also going to bring "Wuthering Heights" by Charlotte Bronte, although I have already read it. Mama said that she doesn't know how long it will be until we can return to Tsarkoe Selo. I suppose we can't return until the Revolution is over.

Mama has instructed us to sew our diamonds and pearls into our petticoats and the lining of our dresses. We all have been feverishly at work with our needles, Mama included. Our time is limited as we can only sew when we're sure that we will not be caught by one of the soldiers.

We are all worried about Alexis. He is not really fit to travel right now. Doctor Botkin appealed to Colonel Kobylinsky to give us more time, but he is insistent that we must leave the palace tonight. He told us to be ready by midnight; a car will pick us up at that time to transport us to the railway station. Sorry I can't write more, Nina, I just don't have the time.

14 August 1917

I am writing this on the first part of our trip. We are on a train without a known destination. Colonel Kobylinski still refuses to tell us where we are going, although Papa has asked him several times.

Our journey has been somewhat comfortable so far, but it is long and tedious. Mama's lips are constantly moving so we know that she is deep in prayer. Papa sits in a stony silence except when we say something in an attempt to cheer him up, then he smiles gently.

Colonel Kobylinsky had told us that a car would pick us up at midnight, but in fact it didn't arrive until about 6 o'clock this morning. We had fallen asleep on our beds with our traveling cases lined up near the front door of the palace. Our heavy coats were atop the cases and so were we, at one point. However, when two o'clock had come and gone and the car didn't arrive, Colonel Kobylinsky told us to go and lie on our beds fully clothed so we would be ready to leave at a moment's notice.

Everyone who was at the palace was given the choice to remain with us or to leave. There were many tears as one by one we bid goodbye to all our household staff. Monsieur Gilliard and Doctor Botkin are allowed to accompany us to our unknown destination.

I especially feel sorry for Doctor Botkin as he is leaving both Gleb and Tatiana behind. He didn't even get a chance to say goodbye to them, but was merely permitted to send them a note saying that he was leaving with us but didn't know where we were going. Colonel Kobylinsky read the note before one of the soldiers left to deliver it.

Oh, Nina, this all seems like a bad dream again. I want to shake myself awake but it does no good. The nightmare still goes on!

18 August 1917

We traveled on the train for three days. Today we arrived in a town called Tiumen. We are all so weary from this trip. There were times when I saw Marie and Olga crying. Tatiana, who seems to be very matter of fact about all of this, keeps assuring us that this trip is for our protection and that anything has to be more favorable than being under arrest in our own palace.

We finally boarded a boat that, at this very moment, is taking us up the river Kama. The boat is crowded with people of such low state that Papa constantly fears for our safety. Drunkards, military men, and peasant women and children are all traveling with us.

We were given only two cabins for all of us. Papa, Alexi, Doctor Botkin and Monsieur Gilliard stay in one cabin and we women in another. Sparse meals of stale bread and broth are brought to us three times a day. We are not allowed to leave the cabin except to use the water closet [bathroom], and even then, one of Colonel Kobylinsky's men escorts us. Once in a while, the Colonel, with a few of his soldiers, guards us while we take some exercise on the deck of the boat, but this has only happened once. A little while ago, I overheard Papa ask the Colonel why, if he and his soldiers were here to protect us, do we feel that we are his prisoners rather than under his protection.

"But, of course, you must realize that the people on board this ship could easily do harm to yourself and your family, especially your beautiful daughters," Colonel Kobylinsky told Papa. "Many of the Russian people hold you and your family responsible for all their troubles and would like nothing better than to hurt one of you. We are here to protect you. Only that."

The very worse part of this trip for me is the lack of space to move around because the cabin is so confining. I find it difficult to sit still and must always get up and wander about, except that there is so little space in which to wander. We try to play word games and number games among ourselves, like we use to do when we were younger, but after a couple of hours, we tire of that also.

Mama reads to us sometimes, and whenever I think of something funny, I tell everyone so they will laugh. Like the time, several years ago, when Aunt Olga came to visit.

I had known about the visit and decided to plan an unusual welcome. Before Aunt Olga was escorted into the library, I had sprawled myself on the floor in front of the library door when I had heard that she was on her way into the palace. As she approached the library, Aunt Olga asked me several times to get up off the floor to let her pass, but I merely grinned up at her and rolled my eyes around in my head. She thought this was so funny that she couldn't stop laughing.

"Anastasia, you are always the clown. I hope you never lose your sense of humor." Finally, so as not to make Papa wait for her any longer, she stepped over me still laughing, and entered the library, closing the door and leaving my prone figure outside in the hall.

I not only told the story, but I demonstrated how I rolled my eyes at Aunt Olga, until I had Mama and everyone laughing until they were in tears. I suspect, however, that not all of the tears came from laughter.

22 August 1917

Dearest Nina,

Our boat ride ended two days ago. We were then put on another train for a couple of hours. Just when we thought that our journey was over and we were going to stay in a little town along the rail, we were transferred to another boat named the Rouss. This time we traveled on the river Irtysh for more than a day. I will try to describe the scene that unfolded before my eyes while on deck.

The river Irtysh runs along the Siberian plain, a flat land that stretches for thousands of miles. There is little vegetation and the few trees that one sees are sickly looking. Houses are scattered about on the plain but there are not many people around. Monsieur Gilliard told us that most of the people earn their living at coal mining and that they are poorer than we can imagine.

One time while we were on deck, Mama suddenly got very excited and pointed to a house on the shore. She was choked up with emotion and couldn't speak. Papa told us that it was the family home of our Good Friend, Rasputin. Papa also said that the holy monk had predicted that someday Mama would behold his house; a situation that everyone thought at the time was very unlikely.

Later: We have finally arrived at our destination. It is the town of Tobolsk on the Siberian border. It is very cold here, although it's the middle of August, but I am so relieved that our journey has finally come to an end.

After we left the boat, we sat at the dock with our traveling bags, all of us weak with exhaustion. Alexei has not been well enough to walk during this entire trip so Papa, Monsieur Gilliard, and Doctor Botkin had all taken turns carrying him whenever he had to be moved. We all thank God for these loyal friends. The trip has been made just a little more bearable due to the attempts of both Monsieur and Doctor Botkin to keep our minds off our troubles.

We have been deserted by Colonel Kobylinsky, who left to go into the town a couple of hours ago and has not returned. However, we are not alone. We are never alone. The soldiers are always within a few feet of us and we are not allowed to whisper or talk softly. We must speak to each other so that our conversation can be heard by the soldiers. We are not allowed to speak English, only Russian.

Papa had warned all of us at the start of the trip to be careful what we wrote in our journals. He is afraid that if we write something against Colonel Kobylinsky or his soldiers, and they read it, they will get angry and hurt one of us. I told Papa that I always write my journals in English so that no one in the household except, Marie, Olga, Tatiana and Mama can read them. But, just as Papa warned, this morning one of the soldiers rudely snatched the journal out of my hand as I was writing in it. He looked at the page that I was writing and fanned the rest of my book.

"What code is this that you're writing in?" he demanded.

"It is not code," I replied boldly. "It's the English language. We were taught to speak Russian and write in English," I lied.

"From now on, you will write only in Russian," he commanded.

"I do not know how to write in Russian," I lied again.

"Then, you will either learn or you will not write at all." He threw my book on the ground in front of me, turned and walked away.

I stuck my tongue out at him as he turned his back. When I looked at Mama I saw her face drain of all its color. I know that I mustn't make the guards angry, but sometimes I can't help it. I HATE THEM!!

Oh, Nina. I though the soldier would confiscate my journal; I was so afraid of losing you. I must be very careful to write in the privacy of my room or under the covers.

25 August 1917

Dearest Nina,

This is the first time that I've been able to write in a couple of days. I slept through all of yesterday. Each time I awoke, I was only able to stay up for a few minutes and then my eyes would get heavy again. Mama thought I was ill, but Doctor Botkin said that I was suffering from the exhaustion of the trip. When I was finally able to stay awake and feel refreshed, the doctor firmly told me to remain in my bed for another day. So, I must do as he says.

In the past, Doctor Botkin was the only one in the world, besides Mama and Papa, who would be allowed to give a command to any of us. Now, however, anyone can and does command us. We are no longer Russia's Royal family. We are like everyone else and less than the lowliest Russian peasant!

26 August 1917

I had my first view of the town of Tobolsk today. When we were being escorted to our house the other night, it was too dark to see anything but shadows. Marie tells me that we are not allowed to go outside, but I can see a great deal from the window in our bedroom which overlooks the main street of the town.

Tobolsk is a dismal place to be. I hope we will not be here too long, Nina. We are all curious about the duration of our stay here but Colonel Kobylinsky refuses to answer any questions, so we are all left to wonder.

Dirt roads lead in and around the town and wooden planks are scattered here and there, almost as an afterthought. People live in the most destitute of conditions with wooden shelters for houses. These shacks stretch as far as I can see from this window, but I have also noticed some whitewashed structures. There is one across the street from us, but I only see official looking people come and go so I think it might be a government building. It seems that the government here thinks more of itself than it does of its people.

Papa said that the house where we are staying was once the Governor's mansion. It is hardly a mansion, but I guess in comparison to what is around it, it might seem like a mansion to some people. The house is very cold and we sometimes walk around with our coats on to keep warm. The bathing facilities are not allowed to be used; anyway, no one wants to take their clothes off long enough to get into a bath.

We were told that the house was cleaned and readied for our arrival, but I don't think they did much work to it. Many of the walls have cracks and the plaster is falling down. The floors are not very clean and the kitchen smells something terrible. Someone is bringing us food, but it is barely enough to sustain all of us. We are bored to tears half the time, Nina…I want to go home!

27 August 1917

Both Doctor Botkin and Monsieur Gilliard live across Liberty Street. They live in a house which looks much like our own. However, they do not have a wooden fence surrounding their house nor do they have soldiers in the house with them. They are allowed to come and go as they please.

Our captivity is very trying on all of us. Soldiers of the lowest reputation are always around us. As long as we stay in one room, they seem to relax a little and don't bother us. We can hardly go from one room to another without one of them shadowing us, sometimes even to the bathroom. They are frequently noisy and drunk and Mama is fearful that one of them will take advantage of us girls. I have no fear regarding myself because I know that I am not the least bit pretty and men would not be interested in me. Olga and Marie are very pretty and I have seen one or two soldiers passing their eyes over them. I overheard Papa tell Mama that he will kill any man who so much as displays a disrespectful attitude against any of us!

30 August 1917

Dear Nina,

One day runs into the next. Mama suggested that we do a lot of reading, but I find it difficult to keep my mind focused. Tatiana, unlike the rest of us, seems to have no trouble with this. She has read all of her books and almost all the ones we shared with her. She is almost never without her head in a book.

"Reading takes me away from this place," she told me. "I can escape in these books."

Then she murmured, "I don't know what I'll do when I've finished them."

4 September 1917

Dear Nina,

I hate them [the guards] will all my heart and soul! I am always tempted to spit at them as they walk away but I remember Mama's warning. She said that I must not irritate the guards because they can hurt me or my sisters.

7 September 1917

The worst has happened, Nina!

Alexis and I were talking about the possibilities of being sent from Tobolsk to England. I told him that I am very hopeful because I couldn't think of what else they would do with us except keep us prisoners until the Revolution is over.

Alexis replied, "Ana, you are very silly because you're a girl and know nothing about war and politics." As I was about to reply that I had no desire to waste my time with such things, Alexis jumped to his feet.

"They are going to murder us! Has Monsieur Gilliard taught you nothing about history? All monarchs have been executed when the people have tired of them. There is no hope of being saved. No England!"

The next thing I heard was a crash on the stairs. It seems that Alexis was so upset that he missed his footing and fell down the stairs.

Doctor Botkin has been summoned and he is with Alexis now, trying to do what he can. Alexis is bleeding inside his body and there is very little the doctor can do to stop it.

We must all pray and wait.

Dear God, if you read what I write to Nina in this diary, please let Alexis live. I just know he's wrong. We will be saved. We will!

10 September 1917

Dear Nina,

Alexis has still not opened his eyes. We take turns talking to him, but he doesn't respond to any of us.

Mama had not left his bedside for these three days. She sleeps in a chair with her head resting near his hand on the bed, in case he should move.

We all walk around as if in a trance, saying little to each other, waiting for a hopeful word from Papa or Mama.

Papa had requested that Doctor Botkin remain with us in case he was needed at a moment's notice. But Commissar Pankratoff, the new leader of the guards, will not allow it. The doctor tried to assure Papa by saying, "There is little I can do, your Highness. It is up to God now and not even the Commissar can keep Him from your presence."

I prayed to God today and made a bargain with him. I told God that if he made Alexis well, I would go to holy Mass every day for a year when we finally arrive safely in England.

12 September 1917

Dear Nina,

Oh joy of joys! Alexis finally moved this morning. He opened his eyes and asked for something to drink. Mama was crying so hard, Marie had to hold the glass of water to his lips. We all started crying when we heard that Alexis was better.

Commissar Pankratoff allowed Doctor Botkin to come to our house so that he could examine Alexis again. After his visit, he proclaimed that Alexis's bleeding had stopped by itself and that he would live. He said that it was a miracle sent from God. Alexis must remain in bed for a long time, perhaps until we are moved to England.

Thank you, God, for making Alexis better.

16 September 1917

Dear Nina,

Alexis tried to kill himself! I can hardly believe what he told me but it is true. He and I were playing a word game that Monsieur Gilliard had taught us, when Alexis stopped and said, "Ana, if I tell you a secret, will you promise that you will tell no one? You won't even write it in your diary?" I told him that I would keep whatever he told me a secret.

Then he said, "I didn't fall down the stairs. I purposely threw myself down the stairs, in the hope that I would die from the fall." I was so horrified that I could hardly speak.

"But Alexis, that is a terrible sin. If you had died, you might have gone to Hell instead of to Heaven with our Good Friend. Why would you want to die?"

"I will not let them kill me, Ana. It is nobler to die by one's own hand than be murdered by the enemy."

We talked for a long time after that and Alexis promised me that he would never attempt anything like that again.

I know I promised not to write about this in my diary, but I just had to tell someone, Nina.

119

21 September 1917

The worst part of our lives here is the boredom. Our books are read and we have run out of cotton for our needlepoint. We tell each other stories and talk about things that we enjoyed in the past. We are so bored that we actually look forward to Monsieur Gilliard's arrival each afternoon.

His face is the only familiar one that we see besides Doctor Botkin. Monsieur told us the other day that he has never received such an enthusiastic welcome from us in all the years that he has been our tutor.

25 September 1917

Oh, Nina

Gleb is HERE! I saw him from my window this morning. He was standing in the street, looking up at our house. I think he was trying to catch sight of one of us at the window. I just happened to go to the window at that very moment, when I saw him.

Gleb waved to me and I smiled and excitedly waved back. At that moment, a soldier ran over and I held my breath because he looked as if he were going to arrest Gleb. Although the window was down, I could hear the soldier yell at him, "No one is permitted near this house. Anyone who even looks at it will be shot."

I breathed a sigh of relief as the soldier turned to yell at another passer-by and I saw Gleb slip off into an alley between two houses.

I hope he never tries to see us again, although my heart aches to talk to him. I'm really afraid for his life!

Everything is so sad! What has happened to our life? I just know that it will never be the same again. I wish that I had really appreciated the things that I had in the palace and the people I had known there. I always thought it would be forever!

1 October 1917

Dearest Nina,

Oh, how I wish Gleb could visit with us; it would be like old times. Doctor Botkin told us that Gleb was arrested trying to get here to Tobolsk. He said that it is only through the intercession of the good Lord that Gleb is here alive and well.

We can talk with him through letters that we give to Doctor Botkin when he is allowed to visit Alexis. I think Gleb is getting to like Olga better than he does me and it upsets me a little. He is really my friend and I don't want to share him with anyone else. Besides, Olga is too old for him. But they are sharing letters just the same. When I asked Olga why she was writing to Gleb, she just said, "Why Ana, I think you're jealous. But you needn't be. Gleb and I just share poems. He gives me advice about my poems and I give him advice about his."

I am still uncomfortable with their new relationship.

4 October 1917

We don't often go outside. It is not a place that one would be anxious to go and visit.

Our house is surrounded by a wooden fence that must be ten feet tall, at least. There is a small space between the house and the fence, and that is where we are allowed to walk, with the guards, of course. There are holes in the fence and the passers-by gape at us through the openings and some of them call out nasty and disrespectful insults at us, especially if Papa or Mama accompany us on our walk.

Doctor Botkin told us that there are notices around town that any citizen who tries to help the Romanov family will be shot!

I'm beginning to lose hope that we will ever be saved. It seems that the world has forgotten us. Why doesn't Mama's cousin in England, King George V, help us?

9 October 1917

Dear Nina,

I haven't written in a number of days simply because there is so little to tell about. Each day is absorbed by the next as we try to keep ourselves occupied.

Gleb thought up something that we can do to pass the time. Doctor Botkin brings his sketches to us when he visits Alexis. We write stories about the pictures and return them when we are finished. We are all taking part in this game and have turned it into a contest with Gleb as the judge. When he sends us a new group of drawings, he encloses a note telling which one of us has won the previous time. Yesterday, I won for the first time since we've been doing this and Gleb enclosed a note telling me that he really loved my story, that it was silly but funny. I'm glad he liked it. I think that it is helpful to be comical at a time when we need to laugh and be cheerful.

10 October 1917

Dear Nina,

I try to stay happy, no matter what the circumstances. Life seems so short, especially now, when we don't know what is going to happen tomorrow. Sometimes I really feel down but I try not to let the others see me cry. Papa and Mama are the saddest of all. They are worried about us, and of course, they must be because we are their children and they feel responsible for whatever happens to us. When I have children I know that the same feelings will be a part of me and that I will do everything in my power to protect them, even if I must give my life for them.

Sometimes at dinner, Papa looks so sad. "Papa is sad today," the whisper goes round. "Let's try to cheer him up." We then begin to laugh and tell jokes which often helps to lighten his spirit. When he sees how hard we are trying to make him feel better, his face changes to one of happiness.

"My beautiful daughters. You teach me that although tomorrow may bring sadness and difficulty, tonight is joyful because we are all together. I thank the Lord for all of you."

It's fun to know that we can teach Papa something even though he is much older and wiser than we are.

Later: Mama has burned her diaries, Nina! We all watched as she threw four of them into the wood burning stove in our house. She said that she had destroyed the rest before we left the palace. I no sooner had the thought: how can she bear to do that to all her private writings, when she told us that our diaries must be destroyed, also. Mama discussed it with Papa and they are both afraid that the new government will find something that we have written and use it against us. Nina, how will I live without you? You have become my best friend, the only real friend I ever had. I refuse to do it!

13 October 1917

Dearest Nina,

I discovered a way to solve our dilemma, but it meant that I had to lie to Mama. I had to, Nina, I couldn't destroy you. There is a loose board in the floor of our bedroom. The space is just large enough to hold this diary. I will hide you there and someday when this is all over, I'll come back and find you. I promise!

Goodbye for now, dear Nina. I love you.

Anastasia Romanov

Epilogue

Anastasia and her family remained imprisoned at Tobolsk for another seven months. Sometime in May 1918, they were moved deeper into Siberia, to the town of Ekaterinberg.

On the morning of July 16, 1918, the family was awakened from their sleep and told to dress. They were escorted to the basement and watched horrified, as armed soldiers entered the room. A few minutes later, the entire family and Doctor Botkin were assassinated and left for dead.

In 1922, in Germany, a young woman calling herself Anna Anderson was arrested as a fake, telling everyone that she was really Anastasia Romanov. Since her mother's family was in Germany, she had been searching for relatives who would help her. Instead, Anastasia or Anna Anderson, was thrown into a mental hospital for two years because the relatives that she contacted refused to identify her. This period was very traumatic for her and nearly broke her spirit.

However, sometime later, she was reunited with her old friend, Gleb Botkin. Once Gleb had identified his childhood friend, he spent the next few years trying to convince the world that Anna Anderson was indeed Anastasia Romanov, the last of Russia's royal family. This has led to one of the most interesting historical mysteries and controversies of our time. But that is another story…

Author: Carol Dommermuth is the author of six biographies for young adults. She lives outside of New York City.

If you'd like to learn more about Anastasia and her family, go to www.caroldommermuth.com or http://caroldommermuth.blogspot.com to find a list of additional books about Anastasia and more information about the Romanov family.

Made in the USA
Charleston, SC
01 June 2014